# Keeper of All Time

Volume 2 of the 'Keeper House' series

A Novel by   W. E. NOEL

## Foreward

This novel, number two in the series, is based on the fictitious
murder of the Keeper Family early in the 20th century.
All of the characters, names and events in this book
are fictitious, and any resemblance to actual persons,
living or dead, is purely coincidental.

ISBN: 978-0-9981961-0-7
© 2016  NOEL & COMPANY

With love and gratitude to my wife, children and
family who have always shown me I could be
more than I thought I could be.

# CHAPTER 1

What a mess!

Bodies pushing me!  People shoving me!

A flood of taxis not moving forward on the streets. It's not that I hate New York City; I actually enjoy its' vibrant tempo, great architecture, fabulous shopping opportunities, and delicious eateries. It is simply that I hate to have to come here from Bridgeport, Connecticut and battle everything and everyone. Every time my employer, the 1st Trust & Savings Bank of New York, has me attend a management meeting, it is always a test of endurance and patience.

I remember driving here for my first meeting, and thinking to myself, "oh, Johnny Hamilton, what a mistake this is!" The drive from Bridgeport wasn't bad, but only the criminally insane try to drive in New York City. A mass of vehicles, mostly taxicab yellow in color, going every direction at the same time. Each trip thereafter, I vowed to take the train. Nice, leisurely train ride where I can read the newspaper, do work, or try to catch a short nap. I really liked it when my wife, Sally, was able to make the trip with me, but with three kids now, those days are gone, for a while.

While in New York City, I always try to have at least one dinner with my sister, Carla Walker, and her husband Carl. Carla is so busy with her research, that few of the family members get to see her, or her husband. Carla is a chemist who has been conducting research for several life-saving drugs recently, and spending time traveling from laboratory to laboratory reviewing key projects. Her husband, Carl, a vice president with Citicorp, handles large-dollar loans to mega-corporations and foreign governments. They are the typical couple that spends all their 'free time' at work; devoting hours upon hours to their jobs.

I decided after my second child was born, that I had climbed the ladder of success about as high as I needed, and whatever free time I might have will be devoted to my wife and children. I have become a family man; a family man who would rather spend evenings playing games with my children, or talking with my wife, than reviewing financials at the office. That is not to suggest that I do not do my job. I have been very, very successful in bringing new business to the bank. I have also raised customer satisfaction with the bank's services, up to a new, all-time, high level. And, it cannot be said I never bring work home with me, it's just that, when I do, it gets my full attention after more important things at home.

Today is an exceptional day in the City, though, with clear, blue skies and temperatures that promise to be in the upper 50's. Days like today make walking downtown enjoyable, except for the crowds of people that I have to navigate. Days like today are great days to spend in the park with the kids. Except, that today I am not in Bridgeport, I am in New York City and will be spending most, if not all, day in a conference room with other people, talking about the financial future for a couple million people. A financial future which I was also carefully crafting for me and my family.

Walking along 43$^{rd}$ Street, I make a turn onto 3$^{rd}$ Avenue to go over one block to 44$^{th}$ . I like this area of New York City and the mix of hotels, foreign consulates, eateries and other type businesses. There isn't anything exactly like this in Bridgeport. Just then I realized I was in the block that always made me chuckle; standing in front of Muldoon's Irish Pub, and looking across 3$^{rd}$ Avenue at a Starbuck's coffee place. I wondered how many people got blasted at Muldoon's, only to stagger across 3rd to get some sobering jolts of caffeine at Starbuck's. Well, the humor of it all was within me, and no one else.

As I started to cross 3rd Avenue, a huge, hulk-of-a-man came plowing through our group of people at the corner, knocking down several of them. I went spiraling sideways a couple of feet, but managed to keep my balance. One fellow went down on the sidewalk only to bounce back up while yelling obscenities at the guy plowing through everyone. The human train wreck never slowed down or looked back to apologize, only continued on down 44th Street as people were pushed left and right. Well, I had seen people in a hurry before, but this joker took being in a hurry to a whole new level. People on the streets of New York City are ALWAYS in a hurry, but not like that fellow.

I continued down 44th Street until I saw a large group of people sprawled all over the sidewalk; businessmen, women, an elderly woman with a large black purse, and one man who seemed to have some type of injury. I could not see the injured man clearly from the back as more and more people gathered around him. He appeared to be receiving some type of medical attention that he needed. The older woman apparently was a doctor and lent her medical expertise to cleaning and taping the man's wounds. She looked vaguely familiar, and returned my eye-to-eye contact with a sort of acknowledgement that she knew me, also. I could not put a name with her face, but I knew that I knew her from somewhere. Perhaps she was once a client at the bank, or was a resident from Bridgeport. Among this group, a young, attractive women had been knocked to the ground and was showing much more of herself than she probably wanted to. The human wrecking ball had made his presence known.

Seeing that everyone had regained their postures, and were relatively unhurt, I glanced around for the human train wreck only to realize that he was long gone. He had either gone down to the end of the block and turned around a corner, or had gone into one of the many doorways between here and there. Time was getting away from me and I have a meeting to get to.

I did notice a lot of security cameras on the building fronts, as well as on the street light poles, and some on metal arms hanging down from overhead. I'm hoping that they are working and someone will be able to identify the human train wreck, in case damages are sought by anyone injured.

1735, nope, that was not my building. So I continued on another hundred feet, or so, to 1747 44th Street and went through the huge brass and glass double doors. I smiled and waved at the security guard standing duty in the entrance, and got a wave and smile in return. I entered one of the old brass-door elevators, and pushed the button for the 9th floor. The elevator made its' way upward with several creaking noises which made me wonder about its' age and mechanical condition.

When the elevator stopped, I exited and immediately stopped at the first desk. "Good morning, Amy," I said with a big smile. "You are looking fabulous today. Even the beautiful weather outside isn't a match for you." Amy had been the executive floor receptionist for nearly fifteen years, and always had a pleasant personality, except when your name was not on her listing of appointments for the day. Amy smiled in return and asked me, once again, why I was so happy on a work day in New York.

"It has to be your charming personality, Amy. That's what brings out the best in me," I laughingly replied. "Are the others here? In the conference room?"

These company meetings always follow the same format: greetings, introductions of new employees (if any), congratulations to best performing bank branches, Q&A session, summation by top officials, adjournment to Italian restaurant around the corner for dinner. However, as I stirred my 'Breakfast' tea, my boss, and mentor, Sol Grossman, motioned me to join him in the outer hallway.

Sol and I exchanged pleasantries about families, the weather, and the trip from Bridgeport to NYC, before he told me that the Board was discussing acquisition offers from a foreign financial company. Sol said that the same firm is also negotiating with a west coast, and a mid-America financial firm for acquisition.

Sol let me know that other than the Board of Directors, I am the only employee who knows of this going on. He asked me to keep this very confidential and not even say anything to Sally until things are more definite. I assured Sol that I would, and thanked him for his trust in me by giving me somewhat of a 'heads-up'.

The meeting went according to plan and no mention was made to the other attendees about the 'talks' that were going on. I always enjoyed listening to Sol's parts of the meeting because of his way with words, and a very dry sense of humor. Sol always has had the ability to insult someone in such a manner that they rarely even realized that they were being insulted. Plus, he has a brilliant mind and genuinely likes people. Honest people.

The meeting recessed for a lunch break and everyone walked down the back stairs to a banquet room on the floor below.

After eating, I felt as though I needed to walk around the block to help settle my stomach. I checked my watch, determined how much time I had, and took off for the elevator. The new manager from the Springfield branch caught up with me and asked if I was going for a quick walk; and, if I was, could he go with me. This was only his second time in New York City, and he still was not comfortable with where everything was at; nor how to find his way back to the bank building. I told him that he would be welcomed to come along, and, maybe together, the two of us might not get lost.

We walked in the bright sunshine and gentle breezes that blew down each street and around every corner. The branch manager's name is Sumner Adams, and he is originally from Georgia. Married with 3 children, his wife felt so out of place living in Massachusetts that she was contemplating returning to Atlanta. His in-laws tried everything possible to get Sumner and his wife and children to stay in the south, but Sumner saw more opportunity with 1st Trust & Savings Bank for advancement and growth. His wife saw it differently. As we walked, I got to know Sumner more, and more, and by the time we returned to the bank's office building, we were laughing and relating some of our stories from college.

When the meeting had concluded, Sol, and Morton Hamlish led the group out of the conference room and through the, now empty, outer offices.

Sumner asked me if he could sit with me at dinner since we had gotten along so well during our walk earlier.

"Of course," I said as we left the conference room.

The train ride home to Bridgeport was time for me to think and contemplate what my possible future would be. I have been assured by Sol Grossman, the President of 1st Trust & Savings Bank that I would be 'taken care of' if this merger/acquisition goes through; but I still have worries; worries about being relocated to a different city, worries about uprooting the kids and taking them away from their friends and schools, and worries about what the overall effect upon my family could be. I kept running different scenarios through my head and coming up with more, unanswered questions. Well, everyone had to wait and see; step one had to occur before step four. I knew that I would have a very, very difficult time NOT saying something to my wife, Sally. As much as I trusted, and loved her, she had earned the reputation of not being able to keep a secret; and, secrecy was of paramount importance right now. All Sally had to do was to let something slip to her girl friends, and the whole world would know almost immediately. Nope, nothing can be said.

The house was dark and quiet when I got home, except for one lamp left on in the living room by Sally. Sally's grandfather clock was chiming its' half-hour chime to welcome me home. The big, old antique clock stood in the foyer like a giant guardsman without weapons, sounding its' chimes every hour and half-hour. The 'old soldier' was overdue, again, for a tune up and maintenance session from the local clock surgeon. I locked up everything securely, turned the lamp off, and tip-toed up the stairs to the bedrooms. Looking into my daughter's room, I was glad to see that she was sound asleep.; same thing with both of the boy's rooms.

As I tip-toed into the master bedroom, Sally was coming out of the adjoining bathroom. She smiled at me and said, "Hi, there. Didn't know if you would be back tonight or sometime tomorrow. It's almost one-thirty, have you eaten anything?"

I approached Sally and gave her a big kiss and hug. "Yes, the bank had a big Italian dinner planned for us at that restaurant around the corner from headquarters. I decided I would catch the last train and come home tonight. Everything okay?" I asked.

Sally filled me in on the kid's day, and how her day had gone. She said that Stephanie Hunter had phoned for me regarding some sort of problem that they were having with their new Victorian home in Westport. Stephanie did not want to go into detail on the phone, and asked if we could talk at Mr. Walker's birthday party. Sally then asked if she and I could talk more at breakfast. Now, we needed some sleep.

# CHAPTER 2

It is a Walker family tradition: all their children and their spouses, and the grandchildren, get together for Mr. Walker's birthday every year. The Walkers usually reserve the banquet room at their country club in Huntington, Long Island, where they live in a huge, very ostentatious home; a home which became much too large for them many years ago. Mr. Walker, being a man of a certain social level, did not talk openly about what people termed as 'down-sizing'; this is the house where he and Mrs. Walker started their lives together, where all their children were born and raised, and where all their grandchildren, so far, would come to see them. But this year, Mrs. Walker decided to ask Stephanie and Derek for the use of some of their property and have a couple large tents erected for the celebration. Mrs. Walker liked that most of her children were settling in the same geographical area, with the majority of children and grandchildren living in Connecticut. Mr. Walker liked that he could drive from their Huntington location, over to Port Jefferson, L.I. and board the ferry across the Long Island Sound to Bridgeport. Easy traveling, he thought. So Mrs.

Walker hired a company to erect two large canopy-type tents, and added a bouncy house and trampoline for the children. She knew that this years' celebration would be different, she simply hoped it would be better, too. Deep inside her, she also wanted to see how everyone would handle coming to Westport rather than making the trek down to Huntington, Long Island. Mr. Walker knew, deep inside, that the two of them had much too much space around them for their continued comfort. While he didn't talk publicly about moving, he had looked into other areas and available homes, just in case. Mrs. Walker had always longed to return to the Connecticut countryside from whence she came. Mr. Walker talked previously with Stephanie and Derek, about having the entire third floor of their Victorian remodeled to accommodate the Walkers living there. It was a short, private talk and nothing had happened since.

It is an easy drive down I-95 to Westport, but I knew that having three rambunctious kids in the car with Sally and me, would make the miles seem to triple in length. So, we piled everything in the car, and started the drive. The children like playing the 'license plate game', and the 'on-my-side-I-have ___ game', so they endured the 30 minute trip without much conflict or complaint.

Sally and I have always been considered, by the Walkers, to be part of their family since my sister, Carla, married their son, Carl. Extended family, perhaps, but still part of the family. We always came to family functions, just as if we were going to our own parents' house. We participated in holidays with the Walker family, whether a Jewish holiday, or a Christian.

This would be the first time, for most of the family members, to see Stephanie's dream house: the Victorian mansion. We will also get to see the new yacht that Stephanie just purchased for her husband, Derek. Purchased, but not yet able to use because both Derek and Stephanie have to complete sailing lessons and undergo 'hands on' instruction from a licensed yachtsman who will sign off on their licenses.

This is also an occasion when everyone would get to see Dr. Gerald Walker and his family. Dr. Gerald was somewhat of an 'under-achiever' in that he was 'only' an M.D. with a family-oriented practice. His siblings are attorneys, vice-president of a major financial firm, a top physicist, or owns one of the world's top precious metals companies. But, on the occasion of his father's birthday, Gerald, and every sibling, was on equal standing.

Mr. Walker took advantage of the opportunity to talk to Derek and Stephanie, again, about he and Mrs. Walker living on their remodeled third floor; only this time he added that they would like to design and build a house on the corner of the property. The Walkers would live on the third floor only until their house was completed and could be moved into. Mr. Walker would pay all costs for the remodel and the new house, and offered a tidy sum of money for the property that the house would sit upon. Mr. Walker said that the house would be deeded over to Stephanie and Derek upon the death of he and Mrs. Walker.

Carla welcomed these family get-togethers and was always glad that she would get to see and visit with Sally and me. She thought that the idea that Sally and I were treated as part of the Walker clan was great. This gave Carla her opportunity to catch up on the lives and happenings of her niece and nephews. All three of my children adore their Aunt Carla and Uncle Carl.

The Victorian was beautiful! From the brilliant white color of its' exterior siding, to the carved details on the entry door, it was an example of the very best in materials and craftsmanship, and both Derek and Stephanie just beamed with pride when showing people around. It was like one guided tour after another throughout the day. I hadn't noticed that Sally was the only person who did not tour the house until Carla mentioned it to me. When I asked Sally if she wanted to see Stephanie's Victorian mansion she said that she was busy with the children and would see it later.

I got a chance to talk with Stephanie and Derek and heard more about their home's 'tainted' history. They learned, months after moving into the house, that a murder had been committed in the formal living room; a murder that wiped out an entire family. A father, mother, and their four children were murdered there, and the crime, committed some 50 or 60 years ago, has remained unsolved.

In addition, Stephanie said strange things were beginning to happen: A loud crashing sound when nothing has fallen, a horrible, rotting-meat smell, which seems to emanate from everywhere, and no where, and other very strange events occurring. Stephanie doesn't know if Derek is aware of these events, or if he is, he has not given any indication that he is aware. She has tried to track down the seller's realtor, David Jessup, but his office and residence has been closed and looks abandoned. Stephanie would really like to know what is causing the events and how they can stop them. Derek, on the other hand, says that a couple crashing sounds startled him but he was not able to find any cause for the noise. Both Derek and Stephanie are reluctant to have Mr. & Mrs. Walker move into the third floor before the causes for the 'events' can be found.

Even their grandfather clock, a bigger, more elaborate and decorative model than Sally and I have, was not operating properly. The clock is supposed to chime Westminster on the hour, and the Whitting, or St. Mary's chimes on the half-hour, but it is chiming the St. Michael chimes any time it wants to. Stephanie has had the clock expert from Bridgeport's 'About Time' clock shop coming by to work on it more than a half-dozen times without success. It is almost as if the clock simply chimes when it wants to, not when it is suppose to.

None of the other family members were aware of the 'tainted' history of the Victorian, nor did Stephanie or Derek want anyone to know yet.

The birthday celebration went off without a hitch. The adults talked, drank and laughed together, while the children played their games together without fighting. The Victorian mansion, with the 'tainted history' behaved and did not produce either smell, noise, or any sign that it was there. All in all, the three day weekend was just about perfect.

The following week I was back in my office going about the daily banking business. I was talking with customers, calling prospective new customers, reviewing loan applications, and making certain that everyone was doing their jobs with precision.

I managed to contact Tom Kitchen, the owner of 'About Time' clock and jewelry store, and ask Tom to drop by our house and service Sally's Grandfather clock. Tom, who also owns several other businesses in Bridgeport including the local Ace Hardware Store, said he would schedule it for the following day and send me a 'breakdown' on what work he performed. Sally was always happy with the TLC that Tom's expertise did for her treasured clock, and she had known Tom since she worked in town at the travel agency.

So it went; the same daily events without things changing much, one day to the next. I received two updates at home from Sol Grossman and Morton Hamlish telling me that talks were continuing between the groups, before getting a notice marked as "Very Confidential".

The "Very Confidential" letter was the notification that the boards of directors, and the Federal government had approved the acquisition of all three financial firms by the London-based Royal Bank of Commerce.

Four hours later, both MSNBC and the Wall Street Journal broke the story, and my office phone was ringing off the hook. While I was busy doing damage control on one phone call, my secretary was taking a dozen other messages from customers calling about the same thing. I called Morton and Sol trying to get more information, but did not get through to either person.

I knew it was imperative that he have accurate and complete information with which I could answer customer's questions. Also, the bank's employees were beating a path to my office door asking about their jobs. No one had any news except some reporter for WSJ.

Finally I received a phone call from Sol Grossman about the purported purchase of the bank. We talked behind closed doors for nearly two hours before I thanked Sol and hung up the phone. I then called a meeting of the employees to be held after the bank's closing that evening. Everyone needs to know what I now know.

The acquisition has been approved by the Federal banking authorities, and the Board of Directors of 1st Trust & Savings. The deal has gone through for all three banking entities to join Royal Bank of Commerce. I gave the news to all my employees gathered in the main lobby. Royal Bank was also acquiring a banking firm in California, and another in Des Moines, Iowa. Royal Bank planned on keeping everything the same, as all three U.S. banking firms were proven profit-making businesses. I assured my employees that I intend to keep everything the same; that there could come a time in the future that some things would have to change, but I did not know, today, when that would be. I told everyone how much I appreciated them, their efforts, and their ability to get even the toughest tasks done.

There were only a few questions asked; mostly about layoffs being done by seniority, and other similar questions. I handled them as best I could.

"Customers will be asking questions, many of which you will not know the answer to. Best thing to do? Tell the customer that you do not know, but you will get them the answer. Don't try to guess, or make something up. Customers of financial institutions get very nervous when there are any changes, so we need to provide them with information and facts, only!" I told the gathering. The bank's employees can always refer the customer to me to handle.

The meeting with employees was kept short and dealt with facts, and facts only.

Upon getting home that evening I was nearly tackled by my two sons as I came through the front door. "Whoa, guys, what are you doing?" I asked. My 8 year old said that they were practicing football stuff and they needed a big tackling dummy. I just happened to walk through the front door at the right moment. I looked at the two of them decked out with their shoulder pads and helmets, much too big for their small bodies, and laughed. I told them they needed to practice out back in the yard so they don't break anything, or mess up their mother's living room. I promised them that I would change my clothes and help them with their practice after dinner. With that they went running off to their bedrooms yelling out football terms and 'signals'.

Sally was standing next to the range, looking at me as I walked into the kitchen. Without changing her expression, she said "I have been getting phone call-after-phone-call from wives of your employees telling me that the bank is closing. They are asking all sorts of questions that I know nothing about. What's going on, and why do they know about it before I do?"

Were it not for the expression on Sally's face I might have joked about what she said. I knew, after years of marriage, when to inject humor and laughter, and when not to. Sally's body language was telling me not to. "I don't know why they would bother calling you, they should be asking their husbands, or spouses, for answers." I told Sally while she turned to stir something on the stove. "I had a meeting with all the employees tonight after closing, and told them as much as I know of what is going on. And, it is not centered on the bank closing."

Sally turned and looked into my eyes, "And when were you going to get around to telling me about what-ever-it-is-that's going on?"

"About ten minutes ago, if the boys had not tackled me as I walked in the front door. I couldn't say anything before now, because I only got my phone call from Sol Grossman this afternoon. I had to process everything Sol told me, and filter the relevant information from the 'fluff' stuff. I would like to fill you in on what I know, and get your input and feelings on everything. Possibly after dinner, when the kids are quiet?"

Sally agreed and finished getting dinner on the table so the family could eat.

# CHAPTER 3

The following weeks went by without any problems at 1st Trust, but lots, and lots, of questions from customers, clients, and employees.

During this time, the Walkers decided to make their move, and put their Huntington, L.I. house on the 'for sale' market. Their realtor was certain that it would not take long before the Walker estate would be sold, but Mr. Walker tried to slow things down as much as he could, so that remodeling of Stephanie and Derek's third floor could be completed. The Walkers hired an architectural firm out of Boston to design and oversee the construction of their new home in Westport. The new home would be about 2900 square feet in size; much smaller than their 8150 square feet mansion in Huntington. This, to no one's surprise, is what Mr. Walker considers as 'down sizing.'

It was a week later that I got a letter in the company mail saying that there would be a national company meeting in Chicago, Illinois. All management personnel, branch managers, and a short list of names at the bottom of the page were required to attend the meeting. The big problem for me was that the meeting was scheduled to be held on the day when my children's sports seasons would begin. I always try to make it a point to attend the season opening games for my son's Little League baseball team, and to my daughter's Girl's Softball League opener. Now, along with the two other league openers, my five year old son is playing 'tee ball'. I hate to not be able to attend even one child's season opener, but with a new owner, I knew I would be going to Chicago.

Sally was not happy to hear about the Chicago meeting. She knew that she would be shuffling kids around from game-to-game, and trying, on her own, to see as much of each child's game as possible. She also understood that I did not have a choice as to whether or not I went to Chicago. She resigned herself to being a "shuttle Mom" for a few days.

My flight to Chicago was uneventful, which is what you always want when flying. The shuttle ordered by Royal Bank was waiting for me when I arrived, and, after picking up five other attendees, headed for the Palmer House Hotel in downtown Chicago.

"Johnny?" someone shouted. I turned to see Sumner Adams waving at me from the lobby bar. I walked over, shook hands with Sumner and two other branch managers and was asked if I would join them for a drink. I told them that I would drop my bag off in the room and return.

I got my clothes hung up in the much-too-small closet, sent my wife a text message telling her that I arrived okay, and headed back down to the lobby bar to join the men for a drink.

The meetings were not enjoyable. They dealt with staff reductions, costs cutting, and big increases in each location's profitability. The people from Royal Bank were quite emphatic about the changes that were going to be made from reductions-in-staff, to raising profits. No 'ifs', no excuses. One fellow even summed it up by saying that everyone would achieve their goals, or their replacements would!

Sumner and I met later in the lobby bar for a cocktail and to discuss our respective 'break-out' sessions. Sumner was amazed to hear that the most profitable branch in their region, which I managed, was being forced to reduce staff, especially by such a large number. Sumner said that he had been given permission to add more people and to look for a larger facility within Springfield. I knew that things just didn't add up correctly and I needed to find out more about what is going on.

Sunday morning brought intermittent sunshine and high clouds outdoors, and another breakfast meeting with more speeches and talk indoors. Dexter Thornton, the new President of Royal Bank, London, introduced more people from London and announced that Sol Grossman, previous president of 1st Trust had left Royal Bank and retired. His duties were being taken over by Royal Bank's new Executive Vice President of Operations, Morton Hamlish. This news completely floored me, for I know that Sol was not ready for retirement, nor had Sol ever expressed any interest in the possibility of retiring. Now, having Morton Hamlish to report to would present some problems for me. The two of us have never been close in our relationship, and Morton has always fought me on every idea, and we just, more-or-less, tolerated each other. I really have no problems with Morton, but Morton always seemed to have some kind of problem with me.

I caught my flight home after the meeting ended and was anxious to hear how the 3 children's games had gone. I am also anxious to talk to Sally about what had gone on, and is yet to happen. I learned over the years that Sally could get to the root cause of most things and find some good in even the worst situations. An uncanny gift that she possessed that I always envied.

After playing with the kids, listening to their versions of how each child's games had gone, and having dinner with the family, I felt more relaxed about the events of the previous days.

Sally listened intently as I told her about the meetings, the people there, the events, and the 'master plan' that Royal Bank had for me and my branch. Finally Sally could be quiet no longer.

"You have got to be kidding!" she exclaimed. "Are these Brits crazy, or something?" Anyone would have been able to tell that Mrs. Hamilton was slowly reaching her boiling over point. "Why do this to their most profitable branch? Wouldn't you want the branch to continue with what they had been doing? Or, am I trying to be too damn logical?"

I really admire my wife's feistiness, especially at times like this. "I don't know what their thinking is, anymore. Sometimes they do the right thing, other times they go really weird. Did I tell you that Sol Grossman is gone?

"Sol? Gone?" asked Sally. "Why would they let Sol go, he built 1st Trust & Savings." The more I told Sally, the more confused Sally became. She kept saying every few minutes, "That doesn't make sense!" Sally and I talked well into the early morning hours before deciding that we could not get any better understanding tonight. We also would not be able to change anything that was happening without sleep.

I kept things to myself for a couple days before calling a meeting with my top people. I told them about Sol, and the 'master plan' that Royal Bank has in store for everyone. I told them that I have approximately 78 days left before I have to start reducing staff and cutting costs, and I plan to use every hour of it. I reminded everyone that it was a higher level of service that built the bank, and it would be service that kept it growing and moving forward.

I asked everyone in the meeting to keep discussions confidential about what I've told them; the last thing we want was to start some type of panic among customers of the bank. "I will keep everyone up to date with my decisions, or any additional information from Royal Bank."

I could tell the mood of the employees had changed; the solemn expressions on their faces didn't change. They went about doing their jobs while I was out trying to sell potential customers on why they should switch to Royal Bank of Commerce. With our new ownership, I would tell them, I could now offer much larger loan packages for expansion, equipment, or high-tech purchases.

Morton Hamlish kept sending emails asking for my list of employees that I am going to lay off. I kept answering that I am revising the list, again. Finally, after several attempts by Morton to get the list, Morton emailed me and told me that he wanted a complete list of all branch employees before closing that day, or he would be in the branch the following day and fire everyone. Left somewhat between the 'rock and the hard place' I forwarded Morton a list of prospective people that I would lay off.

The following day I received an email from Morton saying there would be a meeting on Saturday in the corporate offices in downtown Manhattan. My presence is required at this meeting. Another weekend that I will miss my kids' ball games, I thought. Sally would have to be the chauffer, again, and race from ball field to ball field to ball field. Guess we should be glad that we don't have nine children.

I decided that before I left for this meeting, I would talk to some other branch managers, and would try to find a home phone number for Sol Grossman. I was very curious about what REALLY happened between Sol and Royal Bank. It would not change the things that would come up at the meeting, but I always liked Sol and wanted to know that he and his wife are doing okay.

I didn't learn very much that was new from my conversations with other branch managers, but one fellow did say that Royal Bank told him that there would be some 'experienced' management personnel affected by the down sizing. This certainly gave me reason for concern regarding the Saturday meeting at Royal Bank's main offices. I decided to not say anything to Sally in order to keep her from worrying about something that may, or may not, happen.

It took me an hour of searching before I found a business card from Sol which had his home address and phone number written on the back. I deliberated for several minutes before deciding to pick up the phone and give Sol a call. Even as I was dialing the phone number I was having second thoughts about what I was about to do. I was really concerned about Sol's well being, more than I was curious about what happened.

The phone rang several times, and I began to wonder if this was a bad time to be doing this, then it stopped ringing and a man's voice said hello.

"Sol? Is this the Grossman residence?" I asked.

"Johnny? Johnny, my boy, is that you? What a surprise! Johnny, can I put you on hold for just a minute? I have my wife's doctor on the other line. Let me finish with him quickly and I'll be right back to you. Don't go away, Johnny." Sol requested.

I was on hold about a minute when Sol came back on the line. "Johnny, do I have you on this line, now?"

"Yes, I'm here, Sol. How are you doing? I've been meaning to call you before now to see how you are getting along. And to tell you how shocked I was when I heard the news about you're leaving 1st Trust."

"Oh, I'm so glad you called, Johnny. I've missed talking to you. How is the family doing? Sally keeping you on the straight and narrow? I bet those little ones are growing up really fast." Sol probably had 250 questions he wanted to ask but slowed down for a few seconds to listen. "Johnny, if I loose you during this phone call, please hold tight. I may have to drop my phone and go check on my wife. She's quite ill and the doctor is on his way here, but I have to listen and, maybe run to check her." Sol added.

"No problem, Sol. I'll hang tight. I hope it's nothing serious with your wife. How is your health these days? Morton said that you were ill, also. You feeling okay?"

"Hell, Johnny, I've never felt better and I've not been sick at all. Don't believe anything that that lying S.O.B, Morton Hamlish tells you, he's the biggest lying fool I've ever met. He's the reason that Royal Bank let me go during the acquisition.

Never believe Morton!" Sol said. "I took a few days off to get my wife out of the hospital and bring her home and Morton turned it into a near dying episode for ME! All I did was take a few vacation days to get her checked out, and home and comfortable. She has had respiratory problems for many years, Johnny. Comes from her smoking during her younger years, and somehow she contracted a bad case of pneumonia, which, in her condition, makes for a very scary situation. The docs at the hospital pulled her through it, fine, and she was doing good until three days ago after our great-grandchildren left from visiting us. She has been getting a little worst each day until today when her doctor said he was concerned and would be right over. Enough about this infirmary, how's your family doing?"

"Everyone is fine here, Sol. Kids are all involved in outdoor sports leagues, and running around like crazy. Growing like weeds, too. The sports activity helps to keep them off the video games and iPhones. Sally is taking good care of me and keeping me from going completely crazy some days."

Sol was quiet for a few seconds before saying, "Johnny, my boy, I want you to take my advice, and take me very seriously when I say that, British people are very nice, very honorable people; but this bunch form Royal Bank are NOT! Do not trust them; do not turn your back to them! Ever! The people that we were involved with during our negotiations, are fine, fine people. They have been removed from the front line and a bunch of lying, cutthroats are running things now. I don't say this because of what they did to me, that's just the truth. They took veteran, experienced personnel and simply tossed them aside like they were old newspapers. They plan on closing many established branches in some real profit areas, and spend money opening new branches in places like New Haven, Connecticut, and small, sparsely populated small towns throughout New England. They are doing the same thing on the West Coast, also. Johnny, Morton Hamlish has turned into one of them, so he will never be a friend of yours. Do not trust Morton, either. Johnny! Please hold on, I think the doctor is knocking on the front door. Please, hold on." Then I could hear Sol dropping the telephone onto a wooden surface.

Several minutes passed, and I could hear men's voices talking in the background. I thought it probably was the doctor and Sol discussing things regarding Sol's wife and her condition. I waited patiently and watched the stream of people come into and go out of the bank building. I also noticed that the 'message' light on my phone was blinking while I waited, which probably meant that Morton, or someone from Royal Bank, called and left me a voicemail message.

Finally, Sol picked up his phone and asked "are you still with me, Johnny? I'm so very sorry about that. It is the doctor and he is checking my wife's condition right now. Still there?"

"I'm still here, Sol. You can't get rid of me that easily. Do you need to go be with the doctor? Should I contact you another time?" I asked.

"Everything is under control now that the doctor is here, Johnny. Tell me about the banking business; tell me about your branch and how things look to you today." Sol asked.

I didn't know where to begin and how to answer Sol, so I began with the 'National Meeting' with the Royal Bank people and how they had given every branch manager a goal of increasing their percentage of profit, and to reduce their number of employees. I also told Sol about my being reluctant to do anything quickly with my people. I had been going out, meeting new potential customers, promoting the bank and its' new, larger financial base, in order to try to attract companies needing loans, but had only gotten a couple firms to move their accounts. I told Sol about the 'command' attendance at a meeting this Saturday in downtown Manhattan. That revelation brought some harsh words of warning from Sol. Then I told Sol about the people that I had 'targeted' on my list to Morton as being expendable. Sol did not agree with my choices, but knew that I was between a 'rock and a hard place' with having to do that. We continued discussing banking business, people we both know, and life in general. Suddenly Sol told Johnny he had to cut this call short.

"Johnny, the doctor just told me that he has to take my wife to the hospital. Her condition is worsening and he has called for an ambulance to transport her. She wants me to go with her, I hope you understand." Sol said.

"Of course, Sol. Go! We can talk another day. Hope your wife gets better real soon, and you take care of yourself. I'll be calling again."

The call ended and I went back to reviewing papers that people had been putting on my desk while I was on the phone. Some were deposit totals, and some were messages from other people outside the branch; nothing of major importance in any of them.

Saturday arrived and I boarded my train for Manhattan's Grand Central Station at the Bridgeport station. I tried to relax and read the morning paper, but I was suspicious about this meeting, and about Morton Hamlish. My fears were not lessened any after my talk with Sol, nor after my talk with Sally. Sally now feared the worst, and kept calling it her 'woman's intuition' at work. She did not like the way things were going with this new Royal Bank group and the way that her husband was being treated. I was glad that Sally never gets a chance to talk to Morton Hamlish, or other Royal Bank management people, for she is definitely most capable of scorching their ears!

I did my walk over to the headquarters building from the station and this time it was without any human freight trains knocking people all over.

Upon entering the 1747 building I immediately noticed that things were different; the security guard was a different person. The guard would not let me continue on without signing in on the 'visitors log' and verifying my identification was valid. "Whew", I thought to myself, "things have sure changed!" That was only the beginning. The guard gave me a plastic lapel tag with "Visitor" in large letters on it. I then took the elevator up to the ninth floor and exited. I was all set to chat with Amy, the receptionist, when I confronted a wood and glass wall with a young blonde woman seated behind it. Without smiling, she asked for my name and business affiliation. I answered her and waited for a door to open. After several minutes of her looking at her computer monitor, she said how sorry she was, but my name was not on the approved visitor's list and she would have to ask someone of authority for their approval. She told me to have a seat and she would be right back.

I looked around the area and saw six straight-back wooden chairs off to my right. I went over and sat on one and waited. It took about ten additional minutes before the young lady reappeared and resumed her position at her desk. She did not say anything to me, but simply started typing on her keyboard.

Abruptly, a door opened and a young man of mid twenties stepped through and smiled at me. He was there to show me back to Morton's office. He did his best at creating idle 'chit-chat', but it was not his thing. As we walked through the outer offices, I looked for any face that I recognized, but did not see a single one. I asked the young man where Amy, the regular floor receptionist, was moved to. He said that there was no one named Amy in the offices, so he could not say. We arrived at Morton's office and I was asked to take a chair inside and that Mr. Hamlish would be right here.

I recognized this office; it was Sol Grossman's office ever since I joined 1st Trust & Savings some twenty-one years ago. "Whew", I thought to myself, "has it really been that long?" The office had been completely redecorated and modernized. Decorated in a style that certainly reflected touches of Great Britain, with somber tones of grey, blue, and pale red, and pictures of

Big Ben, the London Eye, and other famous landmarks of London on every wall.

A couple minutes passed before Morton walked through the office doors. He had a big smile on his face as he shook hands with me. "How was the train ride down here?" Morton asked. "Have a chance to read your paper?"

I acknowledged that the train was enjoyable, as usual, but I noticed a lot of changes when I got to the offices. I commented on the new security guards, and sign-in system at the front door. "I also did not see Amy, the receptionist, when I got out of the elevator." I added. "Was she moved to another position?"

Morton sat down in his executive leather chair and smiled at me saying "Amy, along with several other employees have either retired from the company, or have left to find jobs elsewhere. Many of the old 1st Trust & Savings people found that they could not co-exist with the rules and expectations of Royal Bank. Amy was given a nice 'severance package' for her years of service."

I thought about what I had just been told for only a few seconds before saying, "Oh, I missed Amy's big smile when I stepped off the elevator, and was surprised by even more security measures in the lobby."

Morton went on to explain that, in this day and age, no one could be TOO cautious, or be less secure with their surroundings. He said he had met some executives from the firm next door, Sorrabon Publishing, and looked at their elaborate security systems. He knew, then, that Royal Bank had to change their somewhat 'open door' habits, and create additional levels of security. He went on telling me about some of the future additions that they will be making to security, both here, and on the branch level. Morton also said that he had received my list of employees with the proposed people for upcoming layoffs.

"I don't agree with your decisions, at all. I think you have tagged people who are newer employees, therefore a lower cost to the firm, and ignored more senior, higher salary, and more benefits, employees who represent a much higher cost factor to us."

I was really struggling with keeping myself under control and not reacting to Morton's words and attitude. I was amazed that Morton was ignoring a person's value and a good employee, and only looking at them as a cost factor. I was finding this very appalling. "Well, the bank's reputation, which is what attracts new customers, as well as keeping our older customers, was built on superior services. You don't immediately provide superior services with new, somewhat inexperienced, personnel. The experienced people know what customers want and how to provide it."

"Johnny, you're talking about yesterday. We need to staff for today and to start training for tomorrow. We need to lower costs so that we can provide even more, even better services. We need to let the older employees go and hire younger replacements. We may lose one or two customers by doing this, but we will gain dozens more. Out with the old, and in with the young."

"Like you did with Sol?" I asked, knowing that I had just made a wrong statement at a bad time.

"Sol chose to retire, to be at home with an ailing wife. He felt that his retirement time had come and welcomed the opportunity." Morton added.

I was about to really open my big mouth and let my anger take over my self-control when a loud knock on the door interrupted both me and Morton. A young man opened the door slightly and stuck his head in, saying, "Mr. Hamlish, please excuse this interruption but we have an emergency phone call coming in for Mr. Hamilton. It's the Bridgeport police department and they say it's important." With that the young man opened the door fully to allow me to exit.

I followed the young man to an empty desk where the man signaled to someone to put the phone call onto that extension. I could feel my face change during the following 3 to 4 minutes of listening; from someone just listening, to someone very, very concerned about what was being said by the other person. I quickly lost all color in my face as the phone call went on. "Is she alive?" I asked. With that a hush came over the outer office and people were trying to eavesdrop, without being obvious.

Finally I said to the caller, "I'll be right there. I'm getting the next train, or something. What's her room number." I tried to look stoic and not wipe the small tear away from my left eye. "Oh, I see. Okay, I'm on my way. Thank you." With that, I very slowly hung up the phone and just stood staring at it. I stood there for a couple minutes not saying anything to anyone, or looking at anyone in the office. Finally, I turned and walked rapidly to Morton's office. I knew that I had stopped breathing for quite some time and now tried to regain my regular breathing pattern.

When I reached the office doorway, Morton asked me if everything was okay. "No", I said, "My wife and children were going to one of the kid's ball games, and some drunk driver 'T-boned' them in her van and one of my kids did not survive, the other two are in critical condition, and my wife is near death. No, Morton, everything is not okay." I reached down for my attaché to leave.

"Well, I'm, of course, sorry to hear that. We'll finish our meeting and then you can leave." Morton said.

"No! Morton. I'm leaving now! This meeting is finished." I said, grabbing my attaché and walking out of Morton's office.

Morton chased me down the short hallway between his office and the outer offices. "Johnny, we are not done yet. If you leave now, it will reflect very badly upon you. Johnny, come back here!"

I practically ran back to Grand Central Station and checked for the next northbound train departure time. I saw that a train was leaving in seven minutes. I knew that I couldn't make it through the long line of people waiting to buy tickets, and get on board in seven minutes. I saw a phone booth in the corner of the ticket area, and had an idea. I got chills up and down my spine with what I was thinking, but I had to do something.

I went into the phone booth and called Grand Central Station's security office. I informed the person answering that I had just witnessed a strange looking man put some sort of backpack up under the train sitting on track 14. That was the train that I needed to catch. I told security that I could describe the man, but...

With that I let the phone call end abruptly. I then made sure that no one saw me and ran to get in line to buy my ticket. About three minutes later, an announcement came over the PA system that the northbound train to Connecticut, and points north would be delayed due to mechanical problems, and would leave fifteen minutes later.

I wasn't proud of what I had done, but being pragmatic about the situation, my actions served their purpose.

As I was putting my ticket into my inside coat pocket, I turned to see two police officers checking out the phone booth in the corner of the room. I glanced at the large clock on the wall, and hurried out to track 14.

I caught my train, which left fifteen minutes late, and  rushed off of it at the Bridgeport station.

Finding my car in the parking lot, I tossed my attaché into the back seat, gunned the engine and headed directly for the hospital.

I kept telling myself to calm down, and drive responsibly so that I don't hit someone and hurt them. I slowed down slightly, but quickly had the car back up to a 'slightly' illegal speed.

I have never hated traffic signals before, but today, under these circumstances, I am hating each and every traffic signal that hampered my forward progress.

# CHAPTER 4

I detest hospitals. No, actually I detest any, and all, medical environments. They all smell the same, they all look the same, and any and all give me chills throughout my body. It was all I could do to go into the 'Urgent Care' facility that Sally took me to when I slid into third base in a softball game, and broke three toes on my left foot. Here at the St. Vincent's Medical Center, my dislikes were even greater. Nothing about this place made me feel comfortable; not the décor, not the people, not even the variety of aromas I was experiencing. They all seemed to be the same: they all represented death or extreme health conditions, and they all had the same characteristic smell of blood, sweat, harsh cleansers, floor wax and anesthetics.

I stopped at the front desk, identified myself and asked what rooms my family members were in. An elderly woman with a 'volunteer' vest on, checked her computer monitor. A moment later she told me that she would have someone here in just a minute. Once again, I asked for the room numbers for my family members.

A minute later, a man in a white coat with the name 'Darrel Chambers, M.D.' embroidered on it came to meet me. He introduced himself and said that he would escort me back to see my family members, but, first he had to talk to me. Seems Dr. Chambers had been selected to bring the bad news to me about each of my family members.

The doctor explained that my five year old son, Billy, is in critical condition, fighting for his life with huge blood losses and a crushed skull. The prognosis was not favorable. My six year old daughter, Shelly, was in a medically-induced coma to try to get her damaged brain to stop swelling and to drain the fluids out of her lungs and skull. The doctor paused for a minute to find the right words to continue.

Doctor Chambers looked directly into my eyes when he started telling me that my eight year old son died in the crash. He never had a chance because right before the impact, he had taken his seat belt off to retrieve something from the floor of the van. He was dead when the police arrived on scene.

"What about my wife?" I asked the doctor. "Is Sally alive, or..."

"Your wife is barely alive and is fighting for her life. She is in critical condition; has undergone

one major operation already to stop internal bleeding, and has just been scheduled for another to remove bone fragments from her heart area due to crushed ribs. Her lungs collapsed during her operation and we almost lost her then. It will be touch and go from here on."

"I wish I had better news for you, this must be awfully difficult to assimilate all this bad news at once, but there was no way to dance around any of it." The doctor softened his voice when he continued, "There is no easy way to tell you any of this, but this entire medical facility is doing everything it can to help save your family members. Now, when you are ready, please follow me."

As my body ached all over, and it hurt to breath, I was fighting back the urge to let tears flow. I knew that if I did let go, it might help me feel better. I also knew that tears would not help any of my family members get better. I straightened up, swallowed hard, breathed deeply and walked behind the doctor heading down the long hallway.

We had only walked a short distance when the doctor's pager went off. The doctor and I stopped at the next nurses' station to allow him to answer his page. The doctor talked to someone in a very low voice. When finished talking, he told me he had an emergency he had to respond to and for me to wait right here. I said I needed to see my wife and could someone please take me to her.

"No!" said Dr. Chambers. "Your wife is the emergency I have to respond to. She has gone into cardiac arrest and we have to open her up and get her heart going, again, in order to save her. Now, PLEASE, wait here!" And with that, the doctor ran down the hallway.

The head nurse sensed what was happening and asked me if I wanted to sit down and have some coffee. She told me that doctor Chambers, and his medical team would do everything humanly possible to help my wife.

It was nearly three hours before Dr. Chambers returned and informed me that my wife was still alive, but was in a deep coma. They had gotten her heart started and she was medicated to allow her body to rest. Conditions of my daughter and five year old son had not changed; for the better or worse.

Dr. Chambers suggested that I give him my cell phone number, and the doctor would have someone call me when more was known, or my family's conditions changed. The doctor said that there was nothing I could accomplish by waiting there at the hospital; I should go home and rest.

As badly as I wanted to stay, I thought it better that I leave and let the medical people handle things. I felt I should take the doctor's suggestion and go home, but first, I need some coffee and a few minutes to clear my head. The nurse got me a cup of their coffee from a room behind the nurses' station, and then found me a vacant exam room to sit in and rest a minute. She waited until I actually sat down before she left the room. My head started filling with memories; memories of trips with Sally and the kids, dinners with Sally and the way she smiled across the table at me. I remembered the day that we brought a new baby home from the hospital. This hospital. This very hospital where all three children were born, and now they laid somewhere, each one fighting for their lives. Well, two were still fighting, another had lost his fight. Lost, before he even had much of a chance to fight. The tears started to well up in my eyes, but I did not want to start crying now. Not now. Not until I knew more. Not until I knew if there was still hope, or not. Later. Maybe later, but not now.

Two men entered the exam room and identified themselves as being with the Bridgeport Police Department. Police detective Brian Simpson has been assigned to investigate the auto accident that my wife and family had been involved in. I asked if they were able to disclose anything regarding their investigation. Detective Simpson asked me if I had any known enemies. I thought that was a very strange question and asked the detective why. The detective said that "the driver of the other vehicle, a young man named Aaron Franklin, just wreaked of alcohol as if he had been on a real 'bender'. "The coroner's preliminary exam showed almost no alcohol in his system, even though the remains of the vehicle smelled like the bottom of a whiskey bottle. Also, during our initial check of both vehicles, we found some strange electronic gadgets attached to the pickup driven by Mr. Franklin. It's very, very early in our investigation, but there is a possibility that someone else may have been controlling the vehicle that Aaron Franklin was driving."

I let this information soak in for a minute before telling the detective that there was no one that I could think of that would want to do harm to me or my family. I am simply a bank branch manager, and my wife was a stay-at-home mother for three children. No known enemies, nothing that anyone would want bad enough to do harm to them.

Detective Simpson gave me one of his business cards and asked me to contact him if I thought of anyone who could have it out for my family.

It wasn't until now that I noticed that my iPhone had been vibrating in my coat pocket. I took out the phone and saw I had 5 missed calls from Morton Hamlish, and had just missed a call from my sister, Carla Walker. I decided to ignore Morton and give my sister, Carla, a quick call. I hoped that I could keep it together to talk with her. I hit the red 'phone' button and listened to the ring. A second ring, and then Carla answered it on the third ring.

"Hello, stranger, how are you doing?" Carla asked as she answered. "Didn't know if you were still among the living, or not."

Suddenly my voice became quite shaky and my throat got very, very dry as I tried to speak clearly. "Carla, I'm not..." My voice broke suddenly. "Carla, I'm at the hospital. Sally and the kids were in an accident. Things are bad. Really, really bad. I'm not sure how bad, yet, but I've already lost one son." I tried to keep it together to tell my sister what had happened.

"WHAT?" was Carla's reaction. "What are you saying? One of the kids was killed in the accident? Johnny, where are you now? What hospital?" Carla was obviously shaken by what I was telling her. I answered Carla's questions as Dr. Chambers walked into the exam room. "Carla, the doctor is here and he doesn't look happy. I need to go. I need to talk with the doctor. I need to find out more."

Carla still could not believe what she had heard from her brother. "Johnny, Carl and I are on our way. Stay strong and we'll be there as fast as we can. We love you, Johnny." With that the phone call ended and I looked at the solemn faced Dr. Chambers.

The doctor had trained for moments like this when doing his studies in med school. He had to give this type of talk many times before, and realized that each and every time it just got more difficult to do. He almost felt like a victim, himself when he had to tell family members that they had lost a loved one. But, as a doctor had told him long, long ago, he must take the bad with the good.

"Mr. Hamilton, your son, Billy, has gone into a deep, deep coma and there is a real possibility that he may not come out of it. His little body, while relatively strong, is not designed to take as much abuse as it has received from the collision. His brain is just within the margins to qualify him as being 'alive.' I had hoped to have much better news, but I knew you would want the truth. I'm sorry."

I simply sat on the metal frame chair in the exam room. I hardly breathed; I never moved. I didn't blink. I didn't show any sign of understanding what had been said, until I suddenly started crying. And, I cried. I cried like I had never cried before. I cried like a five year old who had just been tossed off his bike and skinned both his knees and his elbows. I cried as if I would never be able to stop crying. The doctor and the nurses left me alone in the exam room and closed the curtains to give me some privacy. My vibrating iPhone in my coat pocket went unnoticed. I just kept crying. I cried so long that I had lost all sense of time. I barely recognized where I was at when I finally stopped. Somehow I had gotten up off the chair and had laid down on the exam table. I just laid there and stared at the blue curtains surrounding me. I didn't hear a sound. I didn't see a soul. I simply stared. I didn't care about breathing; I didn't care about food or liquids. I just stared.

Finally, I heard Dr. Chamber's voice say to someone that he would check and see if I was awake, yet, or not. The doctor pulled back a corner of the blue curtain and peered into the exam room. Seeing me looking back at him, he said "Are you okay? Do you need some water? Are you able to stand up and see visitors?"

Visitors? I wondered why the doctor would say visitors. I swung my legs over the side of the exam table and asked the doctor what time it was. The doctor told me four-twenty. That meant that I had fallen asleep and slept for nearly two hours. I couldn't tell because I felt as if I had been in a train wreck, myself, and was just trying to move my aching body.

Dr. Chambers brought me a glass of water and asked me how I felt. As I stood upright and drank the glass of water I tried to tell the doctor that I felt more like I had just completed a 100 mile desert march with the French Foreign Legion. My throat was bone dry, my eyes were burning and my body ached from head to toes. As I was describing my body to the doctor, Carla poked her head through the blue curtain and smiled. Seeing my sister made me forget all else as I sat the empty glass down on the exam table and stepped forward toward Carla.

Dr. Chambers excused himself and pulled the curtains back opening up the area to much more light. Carla rushed forward giving me a huge, big hug and kiss on my cheek. She started to cry, which made me relive my emotions all over again. I sobbed on her shoulder as Carla cried outwardly. Carl had walked into the exam area and joined the hugging going on between brother and sister.

"They're almost gone, Carly. Gone!" I said. I hadn't called my sister 'Carly' since I was about five and she was eight or nine. Right now I felt like a little boy, again. Helpless; lost and suddenly existing in a world where nothing was right. The group hugging, and sobbing, went on for several minutes before Carl stepped away to wipe his eyes, and blow his nose. Carla eventually did the same thing when she saw a box of Kleenex on the counter in the room.

I finally sat down on the edge of the exam table and stared at the floor. The group went quiet for several minutes before Carl broke the silence. "The doctor was telling us what happened in the accident, and we saw a picture of the van. Johnny, there was nothing left of it. They could almost pick up the remaining pieces with a snow shovel and put them on the flatbed of a tow truck. I've never seen anything like it. Never."

As I was listening to Carl describe the accident scene, I felt my iPhone vibrating in his inner coat pocket. I took it out and looked at the caller ID. It was Morton Hamlish again. I thought for a couple seconds about whether or not I should answer the call before Carla asked me if I was going to answer it, or not.

"Not sure I should, Carla. It's my boss with Royal Bank and we didn't part on very good terms this morning. He is probably calling to fire me. I don't think I'm ready to deal with him, or that situation. Too many other things bouncing around in my head at the moment." By this time the iPhone had stopped vibrating and the call had gone to voicemail.

I put the phone back into my coat pocket and sat back down on the table. "I haven't even heard what happened with the accident I have been so focused on Sally's condition, and the kids."

"There were two police officers out in the front hallway talking to the doctor when we arrived. He told us about the accident and how everything came together." Carl was saying. "Apparently two young men had been over at the university visiting some friends, and had way too much to drink. One young man decided to stay and not drive back, while the other fellow drove a borrowed pickup truck back on side roads to avoid being stopped by the state police. The fellow in the pickup was traveling above 90 miles per hour, the police estimate, hit a kid on a scooter, and while the driver of the pickup was looking backwards at the scooter, sped up and hit Sally's van broadside. He could have been going around 100 when he hit

Sally, they don't know for sure. There were several witnesses to all accidents, so the police have pretty accurate details. The kid on the scooter died from that accident, and the driver who hit Sally just died from his injuries." Carl stood looking at me for a reaction, but I just listened and stared at the floor.

Finally, after several minutes of silence, I looked at Carl and Carla and said, "Good. I'm glad he's dead. He took most of my family from me, there's no reason that he should continue living."

Carl and Carla simply looked at each other without a single word in response.

Finally Carla broke the silence and asked me if I was hungry. Did I need something to eat. How about a cup of coffee?

Suddenly I looked at the two of them, realizing that they had been here in the hospital for a while. "How did you guys get here so quickly?" I asked. "We were talking on the phone and the next thing I knew you were outside the curtains talking to the doctor. Did you fly, or something?"

"Actually, we did, Johnny." Carl answered. "I was with one of my clients when Carla called me and told me what had happened. We were just concluding an early Saturday morning meeting and he overhead our conversation. He offered to fly us here from the executive airport where his private plane was waiting. We never would have made it so quickly without him. First a helicopter to the airport, then his jet here. No security, no TSA. No delays."

"Well, thank him for me, will you?" I said. "He helped tremendously. Do I know this person?"

"Don't think you do, Johnny. His name is Michael Rolden, and he heads a huge hedge fund company in Boston." Carl said. "He's an old school chum of my brother-in-law, Derek Hunter."

I was certain that I remembered the name from somewhere, but right now, I couldn't remember where. Carla again asked about some food, or coffee, or, maybe even a cocktail.

Maybe after I find the doctor and get updated on the rest of my family, I would think about food, or drink.

# CHAPTER 5

Carla, Carl and I went back to the house after I talked to Dr. Chambers. They needed to wash up a bit and I needed to change clothes before we went to get something for dinner.

I decided that I was not physically, or mentally, well enough to enjoy dinner in a restaurant. Instead, we opted for lots of Chinese take-out, and some Asian beer, and dinner back at the house.

The evening went by quickly and soon Carla and Carl were wondering whether to go back to the city, or to stay with me for the night. Carla also got on the phone calling all the family members to let them know what had happened to Sally and our children. Every family member was shocked by the news. No one could believe that our son had been killed. All asked about me, and how I was doing.

Carla and I made up the bed in the guest bedroom so they could stay the night and help me in the morning. It has been a very long, emotionally tiring, physically exhausting day. Everyone's body was aching from fatigue and ready for a good nights' sleep.

I plugged my iPhone into its' charger and noticed that there were 11 missed calls from Morton Hamlish. Also the voicemail indicator was on showing that I had voicemail messages waiting; probably more from Morton. I felt I had a good idea of what Morton was calling about and I decided that I would take care of Morton on Monday.

Mr. Walker received the phone call from Carla while they were looking at some of the remodeled rooms on the third floor of Stephanie & Derek's Victorian house. Mr. Walker was shocked at the news and immediately wanted to know what hospital they were in, and the name of their doctor. Mr. Walker wanted to quietly, and anonymously, do whatever he could for the family. He liked Johnny and the children, but, admitted to his wife, that there had always been something a 'bit off' about Sally. He could never put his finger on it, just that he always felt she was different from the rest.

Sunday morning started off with low clouds and light rain falling. I thought it was most appropriate due to the previous days' events. I still couldn't believe that this was all real; that the things that happened really DID happen. It just didn't make sense that twenty percent of my family had been wiped out. Permanently gone. Forever. Another sixty percent of my family was barely clinging to life there in the Medical Center.

I put the coffee on and then got water going for tea. I made the coffee stronger than usual because I felt my body needed an extra jolt of caffeine. Looking in the refrigerator, I found it well stocked with all the makings necessary for a good breakfast. Yeah, Sally always kept the food provisions well stocked. Very necessary when you have three kids under the age of nine. Correction, HAD three kids under the age of nine, I thought.

A few minutes later, both Carl and Carla came into the kitchen. Carla hugged me tightly and asked me how I was doing. "Okay, I guess," was my reply. Carl suggested that I just grab a cup of coffee and sit down, that he and Carla would whip up some breakfast. I wasn't sure that I was even hungry, but the coffee idea sounded real good. I poured Carl and myself a cup of coffee, and asked Carla what kind of tea she preferred. She said that she would find herself some tea, and for me to just sit down and relax.

Carla and Carl jumped right into getting ingredients necessary for making breakfast, and had everything going within minutes. They worked together like a well-oiled team, as if they did this together every morning. I remembered how Sally and I could never work in the kitchen together; she was always chasing me out saying she would handle 'domestic stuff' because I was a menace in the kitchen. My eyes started to well up, but I quickly grabbed my coffee cup to hide it. It had been less than 24 hours since the crash and already I knew that my life would never be the same. My life, and the lives of others, had been permanently altered by a drunken driver. I began to wonder how my five year old was doing this morning, but I would wait a while before phoning the hospital.

Carla had been talking to me for several minutes but my mind was way off in another world, mentally, and did not hear her asking, "Johnny, do you still like your eggs scrambled?" I finally snapped back into reality.

"Scrambled is fine Sis. What can I do to help?" I asked. Carla told me to relax that she and her cheap help had everything handled.

"Cheap? Cheap?" exclaimed Carl. "I may be easy, but I'm certainly not cheap!" Carl said with a wink of one eye. Carl explained to me that every weekend the two of them were home together they would work at preparing meals together; that sometimes they even made eatable food. He just thought of this as another rehearsal.

During breakfast, the three of us talked about family, who had been contacted, who still needed to be contacted, and when would they start to talk about funeral arrangements. I was not touching much of my food, and the thought of having to handle funeral arrangements seemed to be too much for me today. "I'm not sure I'm ready to discuss that, Carla. Not now! Not now."

Carl agreed; they could handle that conversation later. Later this Sunday, or even Monday. Carl looked at me and said, matter-of-factly, "It is a subject that we will have to discuss. Eventually. You tell Carla and me when you are ready to."

After breakfast, Carl and Carla cleaned up the kitchen and loaded all the dishes into the dishwasher. They refilled their cups, and joined me in the living room as I sat and stared out the window watching the light rain fall gently on the car parked in the driveway. I didn't look at them as they walked into the room. Finally after several minutes, I turned around from the window and said, "Thank you, both. Thank you for coming to be with me. Thank you for coming so fast. I don't know how I would have survived last night without you both. I really appreciate it."

Carla and Carl looked at each other before Carla spoke, "You're welcome, Johnny. We're glad our being here helped in some way. I think, though, that we will have to go home this morning and get some fresh clothes and things, and we can pack bags and come back to be here with you, if you want."

I thought for a few minutes, staring at the floor. I then looked at my sister and said, "I don't want to be a bother to either of you. You have already done a lot, and you both have jobs that you will need to handle tomorrow. Me? I will probably be unemployed come tomorrow. Another knife to the heart."

Carla sipped her tea for a moment, then said, "My current project is at a 'wait-and-see status', and my company has been after me to use up some of my accumulated vacation time. Seems I've accrued almost eight months of unused time." Carl set his cup of coffee down on an end table and said, "Same with me, Johnny, I've accumulated a lot of vacation time that has to be used soon. Besides, I want to talk to you about something, which may be of interest to you, on that matter of a job. I just need to confer with someone first. I can get time off for whatever I can help with." Carl smiled at me, who, at this moment, did not know how to respond.

I asked if they wanted to drive my car back to the city, and Carl simply laughed. "What? Drive in the city? No, way! If you wouldn't mind driving us over to the station, we'll catch a train back, and take care of everything we need to, and be back later this evening."

As they were discussing plans, the phone rang. I just looked at it with a very scared look on my face. Carla asked me if I wanted her to answer it. "Please do, I'm not ready for more bad news." I said. With that, Carla answered the ringing phone.

"Well, hi there" Carla said obviously knowing the caller. "Yes, he's here, do you want to talk to him. Well, he's vertical, but that's about all. Okay, hold on a second." Carla put her hand over the phone and asked me, "It's Kyle Norton, your next door neighbor. Do you want to talk to him?"

I hesitated a moment, finally taking the phone from Carla. "I'm okay, Kyle. Well, thank you...I know...I can't believe it, either. Kyle, I don't want to sound rude but I'll have to keep this short as I have to take my sister and her husband to the train station. They stayed with me last night and have to go home this morning to retrieve new clothes. My brother-in-law doesn't like my taste in dresses."

I listened to Kyle for several minutes without saying a word. Kyle and Sally had both worked together at a large travel agency in downtown Bridgeport. Sally had just graduated from college and needed to start paying off her student loans. Kyle's family had a part interest in the agency, and Kyle put in a good word for Sally with his family members. Finally, I said to Kyle, "That's very nice of you to offer, Kyle, let me ask them."

I looked at Carla and Carl and said, "Kyle said that he was going to run errands today and would drive you to the train station any time you're ready to go. Would that be okay with you two?"

It was agreed that Kyle would drive Carl and Carla to catch their train when they phoned him, and would pick them up, again, when they returned later today. This would give me an opportunity to return to the hospital to check on Billy & Sally.

No sooner had I hung up from Kyle then the phone rang again. Carla answered it and listened for a minute before saying, "I'm sorry, but he is not here right now. He has gone to the hospital to check on the condition of his wife and children and I don't know when he will return. I will leave him a note saying you called, Mr. Hamlish. Thank you. You, too." Carla hung up the phone and smiled at me. "Okay?" she asked. "Yes, very okay." I answered. "He's the last person I need today. I'll be calling him in the morning. Thank you."

Kyle drove Carl and Carla to the train station a little while later, just in time for them to catch the mid-morning train. The rain had started to come down much harder, and the weather person was forecasting that it would be a real 'downpour' today and tomorrow.

I got cleaned up and changed clothes and drove to the hospital. A nurse informed me that Dr.

Chambers was not working today. She checked on my son, Billy, and my wife and daughter, and said that there was no change in status; that they were still in comas and the doctor had performed another 'procedure' during the night to relieve more swelling in Billy's head. I asked if I could see him, but the nurse said he was in post-op isolation and could not have visitors for 24 hours. I thanked her and left the hospital. I brought an umbrella with me and decided to put it to use by taking a walk in the rain. I have always enjoyed long walks in the rain, especially when I had thinking to do. I walked around for an hour and a half, before it occurred to me that I was getting soaked. Regardless of the size of the umbrella, I was drenched. I got my bearings as to where I was, and adjusted my walking so that I could head back to my parked car.

On the drive back to my house, my thoughts were wrapped around things that had happened, and things that had not yet happened. I didn't know if my family would be physically, and mentally, okay. I didn't know if I would be okay.

Just as I was about to turn off highway 5 onto New Karner Road, my car sort of hiccupped a couple times and started acting very sluggish. The first thing I thought of was that I was about to run out of gas. A quick check of the gas gauge showed slightly over half a tank left. I then wondered if the heavier rain that was falling could have done something to the electrical system in some way. I decided to speed up slightly and see what the response would be from the car. Just as I accelerated, a fierce force of energy had my car spinning as if it was on a merry-go-round, and I was loosing all sense of direction. Within a fraction of a second, the air bags deployed and I was no longer able to see where to direct the car. My head was spinning; my car was spinning, the entire world was spinning, and all I could do was to apply the brakes and pray that this would end soon without me hitting someone else.

When it finally ended, I realized that something, or someone had run into my car. I realized that I had been involved in an auto accident, and that someone may be hurt; I realized this, but it still took me several minutes before I was able to think clearly about the situation and attempt to get out of my seat belt.

As I exited my car, I saw another vehicle, with its' front end smashed in from the collision, sitting on the side of the crossroad, Consaul Road. The other vehicle was empty and no one was close by. I looked all over the area but did not see a single person anywhere.

After several minutes passed, a man came running out of a house just south of the road asking me if I was okay. I told the man I was shaken, but otherwise fine, but could not find the driver of the other car. The man approached me telling me that he was on the phone looking out the front window of his house and saw the accident. It was as if the other vehicle started speeding up as he was approaching New Karner Road heading directly for me. Had it not been for me speeding up at the same time, the other car would have hit me just about in the driver's side door, rather than hitting the rear tire area of my car.

I asked the man if he saw the driver get out of his car and leave. The man replied that no one was behind the wheel of the other car. He said he saw the entire event, and that the other car was somehow being controlled remotely. The man said that he ended his phone call and phoned the police to report the accident before he came to check on me.

Both the police and an ambulance arrived within seconds of each other. The police started handling the minor traffic that was building up as the medical techs were tending to my minor cuts and checking my BP and other vitals.

The police took the man's eyewitness report of what he saw, and then took my statement about what I believed happened. They asked if I would submit to a blood test to see if I had consumed any alcoholic beverages. I said 'of course' I would.

The police radioed for a tow truck to tow my car to a body shop to get repairs done. It appeared to the officer heading up the investigation that I had 'accidently' avoided more serious injury by speeding up at the precise moment that the other car did. Otherwise, I would have been hit exactly, as the witness had guessed, in the driver's side door. I explained to the officer that it was not by plan that I sped up at that moment, it was because of my car acting sluggish.

I rode to the auto dealer with the tow truck operator and got my car situated for the needed body repairs. I called my insurance agent and got him involved before making arrangements for a rental car for the next few days.

Then, it was off to my house, a nice hot shower, and a couple of Advil, to erase some of the aches in my body, and then a hot cup of coffee.

The following days went by in a blur; Carla and Carl worked with me regarding the arrangements for the funeral. Other members of the Walker family came up to Bridgeport to help me with whatever needed doing. Even Kyle Norton and his wife came over to cook dinners and to clean and straighten up the house. Everyone was happy to be helping me get through this difficult time.

I called Morton Hamlish as I said I would, and got the message I expected to hear. "Johnny, you were a good employee at one time, but lately you have had your head elsewhere. Some other place, other than your job, your responsibilities, and your duties to Royal Bank of Commerce. We therefore are relieving you of any further employment at Royal Bank. Please meet Sumner Adams at the branch to collect your few personal belongings, and to turn in your keys and other company property. Any questions regarding this message, do not contact me, please call our HR department. Thank you." I thought that Morton Hamlish certainly did not have a way with words; easy to understand why he is the new boss/hatchet man. As I prepare to bury one  son, it is my wife and my other two children who are near death that I am concerned about, not with Morton, or with Royal Bank.

Thanks to Carl and Carla, the funeral went off perfectly. The funeral home did not have a large enough facility to handle the large number of attendees, so the civic auditorium was used without any charges for the family. Compliments of city officials who know me from the bank.

While all the preparations were going on, my six year old daughter passed away. She, along with Sally, had gotten the most damage to their bodies and heads. Doctors had to operate three times in attempts to lessen the swelling within her head, but she finally succumbs to cerebral herniation complications. Now we must plan for a second funeral.

Family members came, along with friends of both Sally and I, our sons and daughter, as well as members of our children's sports teams. There were literally thousands of people. Television reporters for networks in Hartford, Connecticut, and in New York City picked up the story line before the funerals, which led to even more interest. A producer for 60 Minutes contacted me to ask about a meeting to get the story for use in a segment about 'drunk driving'.

I could hardly believe the outpouring of love and support that I was getting from everyone; from everywhere. Mr. & Mrs. Walker had made arrangements with the hospital to pay all of the medical bills which were not covered by insurance. Other Walker family members were making offerings to Sally and my church in our names, as well as offering financial help to me directly. Seems the entire world had heard about my mistreatment by Royal Bank and no one liked it; nor did they like the Royal Bank people any longer.

Andrew Walker, upon hearing of the way that the bank treated me & my family, had several millions of dollars in assets moved from Royal Bank over to CitiBank where Carl had influence as their Senior VP. Dr. Gerald Walker had large sums of money from his medical practices moved out of

Royal Bank, also. The family was accustomed to taking care of its' own.

Amidst all of this, I found the time, and presence of mind, to contact Sumner Adams and set up a day and time for us to meet at the branch of Royal Bank, so that I can collect my few personal things that remained there. All in all, that went very well with Sumner telling me how sorry he is that the firm treated me so badly. Sumner also added his condolences for my losses with my family. Sumner also said that they had not announced who my replacement would be as they were having somewhat of a mass exodus of branch managers. I simply smiled to myself and thought "serves them right!" I looked at Sumner and asked "when you say 'mass exodus', what do you mean?"

"One-third of the mid-America branch managers have already left or have given their notices to leave. On the west coast, it's about the same with some very prominent people going to Bank of the West, and B of A." Sumner answered.

I thought that was very interesting information, but offered no response. I didn't know how far I could trust Sumner, so I thought that the less said, the better.

It did not take long for me to collect my few personal belongings, turn over bank keys and my book of bank codes to Sumner. After Sumner checked everything that I had collected, we shook hands and I started to leave.

"What are your plans now, Johnny?" Sumner asked. "Do you have another job lined up yet?"

"Sumner, I had to bury my daughter and one of my sons. I'm not worrying about work now. I have more important things to handle," was my response.

"I'm sorry, Johnny, it's just with your talents and abilities I had hoped that someone would have grabbed you up. I know you have other things on your mind, and, again, I am sorry."

I quickly left my old office and stopped to say goodbye to the two remaining employees that I saw and that I knew. I couldn't believe how many empty desks, and new faces there were as I glanced around the bank. Oh well, it was not my worry any longer. My worries were at the hospital, and in the funeral home. My worries were much different.

# CHAPTER 6

It has been two long weeks since the services and burial of my son and daughter, and still I felt depressed and lonely. Lots of family members, friends, former employees and neighbors have made contact with me to make sure that I was doing okay, or, at least as good as could be expected.

It was out of respect for me and what I was going through, that Carl Walker did not talk to me about something that was eating at him terribly. Finally, it was when Carla and he went to pick me up to go to the hospital, and then to dinner, that Carl decided today would be the day. Carl didn't want to rush anything, but he had some sort of imagined deadline that he was dealing with.

Carl had discussed this matter with Carla, and, although Carla thought it was too soon to be bringing something like this up with me, she understood why Carl felt he had to.

The visit at the hospital with Dr. Chambers did not divulge anything new regarding either Billy's condition, or Sally's. Five year old Billy was still experiencing swelling of the head and was having sporadic problems with internal bleeding.

Dr. Chambers explained that every time they would start to bring Billy out of the induced coma, that his body would react violently, as if he was having an epileptic fit. When they thought they had things stabilized, his BP would drop drastically, and they would find another bleeding problem.

Sally, on the other hand, was still in her deep coma and did not give any sign of coming out of it. She was being kept alive by mechanical means only.

It was part of Dr. Chamber's duties to be optimistic when talking to me, and others, but his body language never showed any real optimism. He had contacted other specialists and was getting together a team of pediatric trauma specialists to confer on Billy's status. He would be contacting me after that meeting with an update.

Carla, Carl and I drove to one of our favorite local restaurants for a nice quiet dinner. They knew the owner and knew that they could get some privacy to talk about things.

After we all ordered drinks, and an appetizer for Carla, we talked about Billy, Sally, family, and a host of other topics before Carl looked at me.

"Johnny, I want to talk to you about something that I have been holding off from discussing ever since the accident," Carl started with. "My employer, CitiCorp, wants to expand their banking business. They have already started the expansion months ago on the West Coast and in Nevada, Arizona, and a couple other states. They have asked me to head up the eastern U.S. expansion with new branch locations, personnel, and whatever resources are needed to bring CitiBank into the financial marketplace on a true banking level. I hesitated bringing up your name, especially after the accident, but another VP asked about you and I told him I thought your allegiance to 1st Trust and Royal Bank would prevent you from ever making a move. I now think, maybe, that has changed. My question is: would you have any interest in managing our new Bridgeport branch bank, and, possibly being a regional VP for us and covering the New York and New England region?" Carl studied my face after he finished asking his question, but I simply sat and stared at my martini without showing any reaction.

"Yes! When do I start?" was my response after several seconds.

Carl was stunned. All he could do was just sit and look into my eyes. Slowly, very slowly he started to form a smile on his lips. After nearly a minute and a half, he finally let the full smile form as he said, "are you serious? Because, we are. We definitely are serious. We need someone with your knowledge, and your management skills to make this project work. And, it has to work. Our bank has always been thought of as anyone's last choice for banking services; unlike most other financial firms. We want to change all of that."

"Carl, had it not been for Sol Grossman and my group of employees I had working for me, you and I may have had this conversation a long time ago. When they removed Sol from the Royal Bank organization, everything changed for me. I no longer see the same firm that I helped to build into one of the financial firms that the average homeowner could rely on. Or, that the head of household would take his children to, to start their first savings account. I know that when Sol Grossman left, all of the good ethics, and good business practices left, also."

With that news, Carl raised his drink and proposed a toast, to which Carla and I joined him.

"Johnny, I will be on the phone with my people Monday morning, and get a meeting set up as quickly as is possible. Are you available next week?" asked Carl.

"Carl, set up the meeting. I will be available any time!" I responded as I sipped my cocktail and smiled.

After that conversation, dinner became much lighter and was even interspersed with laughter. Carla almost, repeat almost, started thinking that her brother was returning to normalcy. Whatever that is.

I thanked Carl for taking extra time with me before asking those questions. He knew that I had been off in another world most of the time, and I appreciated everyone, especially my close family members for being patient with me.

Carl arranged for the meeting to be held at their downtown Manhattan office building on Wednesday morning. I caught the early train and did my usual walk over from the Grand Central Station.

Carl introduced me to everyone present for the meeting, and the president of CitiCorp had coffee, tea and sweet rolls brought in.

Questions began on one side of the long conference room table and continued all the way around. Carl skipped his opportunity, to allow others to ask everything that they wanted. Even with all the questions and answers going full speed, the atmosphere was congenial and positive. A far cry from any meetings at Royal Bank, I thought.

I was asked tough questions about the economic prospects for New York and New England, as well as questions about where I would locate a new branch in Bridgeport.

"You already have a small branch downtown, are you thinking about closing that one?" I asked.

The bank president said that the current branch was slightly larger than a decent size coat closet, and if they were going to be seen, and thought of, as a major financial facility in the area, they needed an appropriately sized branch. Not a coat closet.

I made several recommendations for the new branch's location, but narrowed it down to a first and a second choice. Everyone looked at each other as if they had just experienced an epiphany.

The president looked at Carl, and then at me, before asking me, "can you work, and function properly day to day, working under your Brother-in-law, Carl Walker?" This question made some of the attendees adjust their sitting positions, and shift their bodies.

"Yes, I can. I can because I have always respected Carl Walker, not just as a brother-in-law, but as a good human being, Also a good financial person with good knowledge of what his employer needs, and what his clients need. Any other relationship we have would be put on the far back burner, so to speak. I expect to be treated fairly and equally. Treated like anyone else, and not anyone special."

The bank president looked around the table at everyone's face before turning to Carl. "Well, Mr. Walker, anything to add, or questions for Mr. Hamilton?" he asked.

"Nothing, sir. You, and I believe everyone else here, knows my feelings and thoughts on this matter. Do we go into executive session, or do we make a decision now?" Carl asked.

"I believe that we are close to a decision being made, but let's let Mr. Hamilton have a seat in the outer office and let anyone here voice their thoughts, first." The president said. And with that,

I got up from my chair, thanked everyone for their time, and went out to find a chair to sit on and wait.

My wait was only about ten minutes before Carl came and asked me to return to the conference room. As I walked back into the room, all the men attending the meeting were, one-by-one, exiting through the conference room doors. As the doors were closed, only Carl, the bank's president, and I remained. We discussed the job that I was being offered, in detail, and what expectations they had for it. Every detail was discussed with me; every question answered, and every possibility covered. When the discussion ended, the bank president asked if we had a deal, or not. I extended my hand for a handshake saying that I was very happy with the terms of my employment and when would I start.

Both the bank president and Carl shook my hand and answered my question with "today is getting away from us, already. You can start tomorrow. Let's get this program going, and let's be profitable. Profits, but not at the sake of loosing employees, or customers."

I smiled broadly, excited with the opportunity to return to the business that I loved, and when I stood up, I wondered to myself what Morton Hamlish, or Sumner Adams would think now.

I didn't wait for the next day to start this project. As soon as I arrived at the Bridgeport train station, I got my car and went driving downtown looking at property. I remembered an old, historic bank building that had been empty for many years and I tried to locate it. In my searching I came across another building that had a 'for lease' sign on it. I asked some of the neighborhood merchants if any of them knew the history of the building because it looked as though it could have been a bank building, at one time. The owner of the hardware store said it had, at one time, been the headquarters building for a bank that had been acquired by B of A years ago. I copied the phone number and info off the sign, and went on with my drive looking at properties.

As I pulled into my driveway, I saw my next door neighbor, Kyle Norton and his wife, walking away from my front door.

"Hi, neighbor", I called out to them. "Looking for me?"

Kyle said that they had not seen me for a few days, and wondered how I was doing. Kyle said his wife had prepared a big dinner and they wondered if I would join them. 'I thanked them very much and said I would love to.

After checking my house for phone messages, and turning on some lights, I grabbed a couple bottles of wine from my wine rack and went next door. I was feeling exceptionally good after my trip to CitiCorp and felt like I was in the right frame of mind for a social evening.

Kyle certainly married an exceptional cook, and I complimented her several times on how delicious the dinner was.

The entire evening was very enjoyable with a great dinner, lots of laughter, some fond remembrances of past days, and some excellent wine that I brought. As we sat enjoying an after dinner glass of wine, I told Kyle and his wife of my new venture for CitiBank. The excitement came through with every sentence, and I told both of them how I planned to build the region up to where I felt it should be. Kyle asked me what would it take to achieve my goal, and I answered "people!" I felt that people make or break a company; people are a key factor in any type of business endeavor.

Upon hearing that, Kyle's wife asked me if Sally, or I, had ever found the trunk that she kept looking for. I was confused by her question, and asked her what she was talking about.

"Several times, when Sally and I would be having tea, or going to the market together, she would have this large, old-fashion key on a gold chain. I asked her about it, and she told me it was the 'key' to all of 'Keeper's time'. This never made much sense to me, but she said that 'they' were looking for the trunk that the key fit the lock."

Now I was even more confused after hearing this. I did not remember ever seeing a key on a gold chain, and what was meant by "Keeper's time"? Why would Sally keep something like this from me?

"Did she say anything else about this key, or what 'Keeper's time' is?" I asked. "I don't remember a key on a gold chain."

"Johnny, I just assumed you knew about this, or I never would have mentioned it. Sally told me the morning of the accident that she thought she knew where the trunk was at. Something to do with her siblings; either her brothers, or her sister."

Now I was really getting even more confused. The more they talked about this key, the less I understood. Time to sit the glass of wine aside and concentrate on the subject. I looked at Kyle and his wife for a moment before saying, "I did not know Sally had siblings. She told me she was an only child, and that her parents had died when she was in grade school. She claimed she had been raised by an aunt who left Sally enough money when the aunt died, that Sally was able to go to college. I wonder what else I'm going to learn about my wife." I let what I was hearing resonate in my head for a minute, than asked "Did she ever say what this trunk looked like, or why it was so important?"

Kyle's wife shook her head 'no.' She wondered if she should say any more, or just let me absorb what he had heard already.

"Again, Johnny, I would not have mentioned any of this if I knew that you weren't aware of it. I'm sorry."

"Nothing to be sorry about. I'm just amazed that a woman I thought I knew so well, that I've shared so many thoughts and secrets with, would not tell me about this key, or the trunk. I'm completely dumbfounded by Sally having siblings," I said. "Why would she keep THAT a secret? Why would she not try to contact them? Or, maybe she did and kept that from me, also." My head was just spinning with questions and thoughts, and unresolved items.

Kyle's wife explained to me how women get into some deep, personal, and sometimes intimate discussions about things that they don't convey to others. Especially when they are close personal friends. All I could think about was how my wife, the mother of my, or our, children, had kept so many important things a secret. Now I was beginning to wonder what, or how many, other things were secrets kept from me.

The more I thought about it, the more tired I became. The thoughts were just wearing me down, and I have a big day ahead of me tomorrow with CitiBank.

I looked at my watch and made a remark about how late it was becoming. I have to be up early, for a change, and guessed that I had better call it a day. I thanked Kyle's wife for a delicious dinner, and both of them for a most enjoyable evening. I asked Kyle's wife to please call me if she thought of anything else that Sally might have said regarding the key, or the trunk. I thought it important that I follow up on what she had told me and additional information would be helpful.

I left the Norton's house and walked around the block thinking about everything that Kyle's wife had brought up, and how could I solve this puzzle I now had from Sally.

# CHAPTER 7

My first day with CitiBank was fast; it seemed like I just got out of bed and seconds later I was walking back into my living room that evening. I met all six employees at the bank branch and held a brief meeting with them and Carl Walker, who came up from corporate to introduce me.

I saw real potential in five of the six employees. I saw potential in the future of their business banking services, but knew I needed to expand every service tremendously.

The next five days went by in an absolute blur. I got into reviewing every individual's account and every business account. I found some accounts that were costing the branch money to maintain due to their low balances and constant upkeep costs, and others that simply had no activity at all. I also saw almost all of these accounts were very old, longtime customers of the bank. I jotted some names and addresses down on a list so that, as time would allow me, I would make personal visits to these customers, as well as the larger commercial accounts. I hoped to be able to visit each and every customer of the bank eventually.

The branch had several customers come in and open new accounts when they found out that I was now managing the branch. One customer even moved all of his business, and personal bank accounts when he got this news. Within two weeks, most people in the Bridgeport area, who were interested in financial affairs, had heard about CitiBank's new manager.

Around lunch time one day, a man came into the bank and asked to speak with the manager. The 'new manager', that is. I went to meet this man who introduced himself as Tom Kitchen, the owner of the 'About Time' clock and jewelry store just two blocks away, and a couple other businesses around town. I had talked to Tom on the phone when Sally's grandfather clock needed some work, but I had never met him face-to-face before. Tom said that he had been at a local businessman's luncheon, sponsored by an area social group a couple years ago, at which I was a guest speaker. Tom liked what I had to say about financial opportunities for small businesses, but felt that the 1st Trust organization was just too small for his needs. Now that I was with a much larger financial firm, Tom was interested in talking with me to see how much of what I had talked about then, might be available now. I offered to buy Tom some lunch and we could discuss whatever he wanted to, but Tom insisted that he had to get back to his store. He had several customer's jewelry pieces that had to be processed, and Tom was the only employee capable of doing this. He called himself "the Key person" in his business. Tom and I spent an hour discussing bank services, fees, and such before Tom looked at his watch and said he had to get back to work. Tom extended his arm to shake hands, telling me that he thought we should schedule a meeting for the following week to handle moving his company's banking business from Royal Bank over to CitiBank. I thanked him and said that I would be available any time that he was available.

Another morning, a state legislator came in with her eleven year old granddaughter to open a 'college' account'. The legislator was very glad to hear that I was the new manager and that I was doing well after Sally's accident. We chatted about a number of things before her granddaughter pulled a chain out from under her shirt. On the chain was an odd-looking key, which I noticed immediately. My thoughts, for the first time since dinner with Kyle and his wife, suddenly went back to the mystery of 'the key' and 'the trunk'.

Later that day I stopped by the hospital on my way home. Dr. Chambers felt that Billy should, once again, be brought out of the medically induced coma he was in. Having his life supported by an array of machines was no fit life for a five year old, but still the thought of Billy having to go through more operations in order to try to save him, was also spine-chilling. Sally was not responding to any treatment that doctors had tried. She continued to exist only because of the machines that kept her alive; clinically alive, that is. Dr. Chambers was optimistic with me, as he had always been, but it was me who was now less, and less, hopeful about my loved one's recoveries.

Heading home, I stopped by my favorite Chinese food take-out place and grab myself some dinner.

I sat down in front of the TV set, chow mein and other delicacies in front of me, to eat and watch the evening news. Some words spoken by the announcer reminded me of the little girl's gold key on a chain earlier that day. I thought, as I downed some Kun Pao Chicken, about where Sally would keep something she felt was so special, like a key on a chain. I watched the news talk about storms, floods and forest fires on the west coast.

Suddenly I remembered a little metal box that Sally had put on the top shelf on her side of the closet. I had not opened it since she said it only contained things from her childhood. I thought I should take a look inside that box, and also look around on Sally's side of the closet, as well as in her dresser.

After dinner, I started looking through her side of the closet. Since her accident, I had not ventured into any part of our house that was 'hers' before. I didn't go through her clothes, or her dresser. I had not even moved any of her cosmetics in our bathroom. Now, I wanted to see what I could find. I went through everything before realizing that I was tired and worn out. I decided that the rest of my search would have to wait for another time.

Before heading off to bed, I needed to put some items in the garage for storage. I decided to go through some of Sally's things in the garage when I saw a cardboard box with Sally's writing on it, saying: 'cosmetics'. I grabbed it and headed for the trash bin to toss it when something inside made somewhat of a clinking sound. Curious, I opened it to see what kind of cosmetics I was about to throw away.

I set the box down on my workbench for a closer inspection. I was somewhat surprised that there were dozens of those 'sample' size bottles of perfumes, lots of lipsticks of varying shades, and several dozen other cosmetic items. There, in all its' shining glory, underneath everything else, was a long gold chain with a key attached to it, and an old Mason jar. Inside the Mason jar was a neatly folded piece of paper; an old piece of paper. I dug around inside the box and found a plastic 'Ziploc' type bag with more papers inside of it.

I grabbed the chain and key and put them in my shirt pocket. I then opened the bag and started going through the papers therein. I was amazed at what I was seeing: photocopies of newspaper headlines about some 'family murder', 'murdered children', missing children, and some people's suicides. Other pieces of paper were copies of birth certificates for a Thomas Allan Keeper, and one for Sally Ann Keeper. Still another listed a Gilbert

Keeper and a female named Helen Louisa. No last name for Helen, and no other vital statistics for any of them. There were two old photos in the box also. Both photos were of the same house, although one photo was obviously much older than the other. The newer photo looked as though it was taken after the house had been painted and the landscaping given some TLC. Several other small pieces of paper seemed to be someone's handwritten notes, but they did not make much sense.

One note said 'key man'. Another said 'medical gotcha'. And another said 'politico – NO!'. None of this made any sense to me, so I put all the papers back into the plastic envelope and resealed it closed. I tried to unscrew the lid off the Mason jar without success. So I padded the glass jar with shop rags and put it in my bench vise. I then grabbed my big pipe wrench and with very little effort, was able to force the lid to turn. I made certain I did not break the jar when I took the lid off. The last thing I needed was to have broken glass all over.

I carefully took the paper out of the jar and unfolded it. I read the words on it, and then had to reread it, again. It was some form of poem, which I did not understand:

YOU HAVE FOUR NUMBERS, BUT THE FIFTH ONE YOU NEED.

SO ALL OF THESE CLUES, ARE CLUES YOU SHOULD HEED.

THE KEEPER OF KEYS, OR SO IT IS WRITTEN,

IS THE PERSON YOU SEEK, FOR, WITH HIM YOU ARE SMITTEN.

I read, and reread, the poem over and over and never did understand what it meant. I decided to put the paper back into the Mason jar and keep it, along with the various papers I found. The key and chain I am going to show to Kyle Norton's wife for verification that it is the one she saw Sally wearing.

For now, though, I was about to throw away a whole lot of cosmetics in the trash bin. After, of course, I double checked the box.

# CHAPTER 8

I met Carl Walker at the property that I considered to be the first choice for a new location. It had actually been a bank many years ago but that bank was acquired by another, and this branch was closed. Since then, it had been a bar, a restaurant, and a flower shop. It had three times the branch's current square feet of space, and still had the original vault intact.

Carl and I walked the interior with Jerry Eldon, the realtor handling the property. I was content to take possession with a good lease, but Carl had been given instructions to try to get a good price for a purchase, rather than a lease.

The property needed a lot of clean up and remodeling to bring it up to CitiBank's standards. The old security system was totally unusable, and the old vault was now questionable. Even with the many uses the building had gone through over the years, Carl Walker could see the possibility of it being the bank's new location. One thing that both Carl and I liked, it was located only one-and-one-half blocks from our current branch location. A lot of customers would have little additional distance to go to get to it.

Carl and Jerry Eldon talked about a number of items in regards to the building including a price per square foot. Jerry Eldon said the owners did not want to sell, they wanted a ten year lease. Carl said that was not a consideration, and asked Jerry to go back to his clients and get a price based on a sale, not a lease. Otherwise, they were looking to obtain a different property.

Back in the branch, Carl and I talked about the property we had just seen, and three others that I felt should be looked at.

Carl asked if he and Carla could take me out for dinner tonight as Carla was on the train heading for Bridgeport. I thought that sounded good, but said I wanted to stop by the hospital, after closing, to check on Sally and Billy's conditions. Dr. Chambers had called and said that the team of doctors wanted to confer on their recommendations for Billy's future care and treatment.

Carl decided that he would go to the train station and pick up Carla while I was at the hospital, and meet the two of them at my house around seven.

The hospital was a lot move active than usual with the ambulance entrance to ER very busy. Seems like traffic accidents prefer Friday afternoons, or evenings, to happen on than any other day. I finally found Dr. Chambers helping the ER staff and once he could exhale for a minute or two, I talked to him about Sally and Billy's conditions, and future treatments.

Dr. Chambers was not pleased with the way that Billy responded to being off the life support equipment, and that he was not getting any increased mental stimulus or muscle movement. He thought the future, while it could be a long and very bumpy road, did not look bright for Billy. Dr. Chambers proposed that Billy be moved over to the hospital's new children's hospital for his additional care. Dr. Chambers would still be Billy's primary care physician, but they will have more, newer, equipment in their pediatric hospital that Billy will need for any recovery. I asked when Dr. Chambers thought this move might occur, and the doctor anticipated about a week to two weeks to get everything set up, and to physically move Billy.

Sally, on the other hand, continued to need the life support system in order to stay alive. She kept experiencing cranial bleeding episodes, which worried Dr. Chambers and others, and she had an episode where her lungs collapsed and the doctors had to perform an emergency operation to expand them again.

I agreed to having Billy moved over to the new children's hospital as soon as it was possible.

"Good", said Dr. Chambers. "Would you like to come to the ribbon-cutting ceremony next week? It might interest you to know that this new children's hospital will be dedicated as the "Montgomery & Eloise Walker Children's Hospital." Dr. Chambers smiled at me. "I think you may know that name."

"I certainly do. I would love to be there. What day and what time?" I asked.

Dr. Chambers said he would have his office email all the information to my email address. I asked if I could see Sally or Billy while I was there at the hospital. The doctor made a phone call, and told me that Billy had finally fallen asleep. Give him two to three hours rest and then I could visit. Sally was in post-op recovering from her emergency operation.

I pulled my car into the garage but did not see another car parked any where near my house. Maybe Carla and Carl encountered some traffic and are delayed. I went in the house and checked the wine refrigerator and got some glasses ready for them.

It was about thirty minutes later that there was a knock on the front door. As I opened the door Carla entered and gave me a big hug and kiss. Carl was following close behind her while talking on his cellphone.

"Well, that's too bad they feel that way but we are not going to lease. I understand that what they are offering is a good rate-per-square-foot, but we will be buying our property, not renting...well, call it lease, okay, it is still rent...if you want to, but from what you say it sounds as though they are firm, and so are we. Fine, you have my number. Goodbye." That was the conversation that Carl was having with Jerry Eldon, the real estate agent.

Carl smiled at me as he put his cell phone into his pocket. "That's it", Carl said, "I'm off the clock now and no more business until Monday morning."

Carla let out a short, shallow chuckle at the sound of that statement.

I poured each of them a glass of wine and said I just had to wash my face and put another shirt on. I asked Carl if there was any change regarding the property.

"Not yet," Carl answered, "But I hope they will process things over the weekend and make a different decision come Monday. The building has been empty for a long time, so they need to consider all options. Right now they are steadfast for only leasing. I have a meeting in the city on Monday, but maybe Tuesday, you and I can go look at some other property...just in case."

I agreed and left for the bedroom to freshen up and change. Ten minutes later I was back in the family room where Carl and Carla were watching the evening news on TV.

"The world still spinning 'round?" I asked.

Carla told me to 'shush.' "They are coming back from commercials to tell about CitiCorp being acquired by Royal Bank of Commerce from London. We want to hear more about this."

I stopped mid-step and exclaimed "WHAT?" I turned to look at my sister's blank expression. I looked at Carl who had moved very close to the TV set and was not saying a thing. "You are kidding, right? Come on! Tell me this is a joke!"

Carla still had not moved a single facial muscle as she said "That's what they said when we turned on the TV. Royal Bank of Commerce."

My spine had chills running up and down it to the point where my 'goose bumps' had goose bumps.

Finally, Carl started laughing and falling on to the floor. He absolutely had lost control of himself with all the laughter. And, of course, when Carl started his laughter, Carla could not hold it together any longer and started laughing hysterically.

At that, I just set my empty glass down on a table and stared at the two grown ups laughing uncontrollably and beginning to laugh even harder at the look on my face.

"THAT, is NOT funny, you two!" I told them. "Not funny at all. Look at my arms, how big the goose bumps are!" I had to admit, after a minute or two that seeing these two literally rolling on the floor, did make me laugh.

"Sorry, honey, I just couldn't keep it together anymore. That was priceless!" Carl said to Carla. Carla admitted that she didn't think she could, either.

"Okay you two clowns. Now that you've had your fun, how about we go get some dinner." I said.

Everyone collected themselves, finished their remaining wine, and left the house for Carl's car.

Italian food was the decision made, while Carl drove us downtown, and I know of the perfect little family-run restaurant.

During dinner I asked Carl if he knew that the hospital was dedicating the entire new children's section to his parents. Carl said that he did, and that they had contributed large sums of money to the hospital. They wanted it to be used solely for children's medical purposes, especially research. Carl thought it might be dedicated next weekend, but was not certain.

I said that Billy's doctor, Dr. Chambers, was going to email me the information so that I could attend. I also told them about the strange key and chain that I had found and how the next door neighbor's wife had told me about Sally's many conversations with her.

No one could understand any significance for the key and chain, but did question the copies of birth certificates, and other pieces of paper. We all started 'brain-storming' with each other regarding the piece of paper with the poem written on it. Carla kept asking 'what four numbers' was it referring to, while Carl questioned the statement about 'the keeper of keys'. Who would be a 'keeper of keys'? Why would someone be 'smitten' with this person? And, what clues are to be heeded?

Carl said this was like some of the assignments that his sister, Stephanie, had received in law school. Give someone some clues, but not enough clues to answer questions, and see what they can deduce. Carl suggested that all three of us look at the papers together and see if we can make something of it. I offered them the guest room for the weekend if they wanted to stay. Carla thanked me and said they would take me up on my offer. Maybe tomorrow, with clearer heads, we could all decipher things better.

The morning brought blue skies, some puffy white clouds, and copious amounts of sunshine. After a good night's sleep, the world looked much better to the three of us.

The coffee was brewing, the tea was hot, the egg omelets were nearly perfect, and only the hash brown potatoes were being over cooked. Carl had only one job this morning: watch the hash browns and don't let them burn! It didn't happen that way. Carla referred to it as "overly well done!"

I set the table and got orange juice made and ready, I also went out to my work bench and retrieved all the papers and notes that we had discussed at dinner the night before.

Carla used a magnifying glass to closely examine the copies of the four birth certificates in hopes of finding some obscure clue. She thought it very strange that the fourth certificate, one for Helen Louisa, did not have a last name as the others did. She also compared the two photos of the old house and gave the newer one to Carl, asking him if it looked familiar to him.

"Sort of," Carl said. "I've seen this house somewhere before, I just can't remember where. It looks somewhat like Stephanie's Victorian, but not as large and a different color. Anything new from the birth certificates?" he asked, getting a "nothing" reply.

Carla asked about the copies of the newspaper articles that covered the murder of a family, some missing children, some murdered children and several other items. I told her that there was not enough of each newspaper article to be able to piece anything together to make some sense. We tried fitting all of them together to see if any of the pieces would divulge any clues as to what the main storyline might have been. No luck.

Carl asked about the reference to the 'keeper of keys' in the poem, and what Carla and I thought about that. Who is the keeper of keys? Why is he important? Why would he be 'the person' someone would seek? Just so many more questions than answers kept us all on edge.

Just then Carl's cell phone rang and startled all of us. Carla's first remark was to remind Carl that it is the weekend and he was to have turned off the phone. Carl looked at the caller ID, and saw the number was his sister Stephanie's. He quickly answered the call.

While Carl was talking on the phone, Carla asked me about Sally and Billy's conditions, and how soon Billy was going to be moved to the new children's hospital. I told her just as soon as they are convinced he is stabilized and the room where he will be moved to, is equipped for his comfort. As for Sally, it was not as good of news because of her bleeding in the skull, and her respiratory problems. After about ten minutes, Carl ended the call with his sister.

"Stephanie and her husband, Derek, are coming up to Bridgeport for the hospital dedication ceremony, whenever it is. Stephanie said that they will sail their yacht here, and stay on it while they are here," Carl said. "Seems they are having some problems with their home that they bought over in Westport. She didn't go into details, just that they have some problems, and the problems are delaying the construction on the new house for my parents, too."

I said that they would be welcomed to stay here, at my house, take the master bedroom and I would sleep in Billy's bedroom. Carl thanked me and said he would tell Stephanie when he talked to her again. Carl also said for me to 'not hold your breath', or, feel insulted if they declined. Seems Stephanie's husband, Derek, as a famous writer, often prefers to stay off by themselves so that he can work.

Carla asked me about the handwritten notes and what I thought they mean. What would the note with "politico – NO!' have to do with anything. Another one puzzled her because it read 'medical gotcha', and made no reference to anyone or anything. I simply shrugged my shoulders and admitted that I could not figure any of them out.

Carl said that he thought that the main clue was the third note referring to the 'key man'. He said that not only was 'key man' referred to in this note, but also in the poem found in the mason jar. The poem referred to 'The keeper of keys', and that must mean the 'key man'. Or, vice versa.

Both Carla and I looked at each other for a while before I said "I think you could be right, Carl. There is more than one reference to a 'key man'. So what, or who, is this person? Is it a man? How is the term 'key' meant to be used?"

Carl said that in business it means a person, or persons, who is key to the business; as in a company president, CEO, CFO, or someone like a top salesperson in a sales organization. If the term referred to someone in business, he wondered what type business, and where they would be located.

Carl could not begin to fit pieces of this puzzle together; nor could Carla or I.

Carla asked what other 'keys' there could be; that maybe we were not looking at the correct meaning of the word.

Carl said there are 'key words' and that an English language teacher, or professor, could be a keeper of such.

Carl said maybe it was a locksmith; someone who has to make keys and is, in some ways, a 'keeper of keys', as in the key blanks that he has.

Suddenly Carla and I looked at Carl, then at each other. Carla could tell that I just had an idea by the look on my face.

I smiled and said, "I had a customer come in the branch a couple weeks ago, and he owns the clock and jewelry store in town, as well as the Ace Hardware store a couple blocks from here. He had to rush back after we talked a little while, because he had to make up a lot of pieces of jewelry to fill customers' orders. He referred to himself as the 'key man.' Now, what if the clues referred to someone like that, or as you say, a locksmith."

Carl thought for a few seconds and said, "I

think we could be on to something here, but I don't know what it is, yet."

Carla looked at both of us and said that all three of us needed to put all this aside, for a while, and concentrate on other matters. She may have been right, but I could not shake that inner feeling that we are on to something; something I didn't understand but knew I had to discover more about. Why would Sally have all this, and put such emotional value on a gold chain and key.

Why? Why? Why?

CHAPTER 9

The new wings of the children's hospital are a beautifully designed structure. The project architects had brought together a very classic style with modern day materials to produce a design that would look new for many, many years. Every department of every floor is equipped with the latest technology; technology that allows parents of a child having surgery to know every stage of their child's treatment via TV sets with last names and current status shown. Even the robotic 'nurses' were brightly colored pieces of technology that the children would not be fearful of. The hospital had an APP developed for use with smart phones that allowed parents to 'chat' with their child's doctor, or head nurse, for updates. Emails could go both ways between hospital staff and parents, and parents could even access the results of some tests via their smart phones. Every department was staffed with pediatric specialists of every medical specialty. The directors had even convinced Dr. Helen Eldon, head of pediatric surgery at Mt. Sinai Hospital in Manhattan, to head up the pediatric wards. It was somewhat of a homecoming for Dr. Eldon as she was raised in Bridgeport and was a graduate of St. Vincent's Medical Center, and a leading specialist in pediatric medicine and surgery.

The dedication ceremony was set to be held on Saturday morning and the local weatherman has promised blue skies and mild temperatures for the event.

A long list of dignitaries were invited, from the state governor, to Walker family members and friends. Even in an area largely over shadowed by events in New York City, and elsewhere, the hospital's dedication of new pediatric wings, was a big event. Local TV stations were covering the event, and even a TV reporter, Janice Wilkins from CNN, was given a press pass.

The day before the dedication, my house was a 'bee hive' of activity with friends, and various Walker family members coming and going. Everyone decided that this would be a perfect meeting place and good place to sit and visit. I had anticipated this and stocked up on beer, wine and lots of snacks. Only Carl and Carla decided to stay with me, which pleased me and gave all of us more room at night.

Amidst all the activity occurring at my house, came a knock on the front door from two very large men in dark suits and ties. Upon seeing the two, my first reaction was that they were selling some religion and all set to dismiss them when the one man introduced himself as Darren Miller, an FBI agent. The other man is his brother, Devon Miller, who happens to be an investigator with the NSA. After checking their ID's I invited them into the kitchen so that we could talk in private.

Darren Miller explained that the FBI was assisting the National Security Administration in investigating a matter which has possibly involved some of my relatives. It was just a coincidence that the two brothers happened to be matched up together on the same case.

Being very confused with all this, I had many questions that I wanted to ask, but let the FBI man continue. "Do you know a man named 'Guido Kiefer', or 'Gilbert Keeper'?" asked Darren.

I said I did not, and asked which of my relatives this case might involve.

"We'll get to that in a minute." Answered Darren. "Have you ever seen this man?" he asked, showing me a picture of Guido Kiefer. I shook my head no. Then Darren showed me another picture taken at Derek & Stephanie Hunter's wedding showing me talking to two men, one of whom was Guido Kiefer.

I studied the picture for a moment, and then said "That is a picture of the wedding of my sister's, sister-in-law a couple years ago, and I have no idea why that guy is standing there as if I was talking to him. There were hundreds, and hundreds of people at the wedding, and the only thing I remember about him is that he was part of the wedding party. I don't know him. I was talking to these other two fellows."

Darren could sense some anxiety building up in me, so decided to change his approach.

"Was this the only time you remember seeing this other fellow? At the wedding?"

"Yes. I didn't know him and didn't talk to him. He just sort of stood there listening to other people's conversations. Why are you interested in him, this Guido something?" I asked.

"It's an ongoing investigation, so we're not able to discuss the matter, we are just trying to gather information." Darren said as he looked out at the crowded living room. He smiled at me saying "looks like you're having another wedding get-together today."

"No, family and friends coming into town for a dedication of a new children's hospital wing tomorrow which will be named after my in-laws. My son, and my wife, are both recovering there from an auto accident several months ago which took two of my children's lives."

Just then, Carla walked into the kitchen and excused herself from interrupting our conversation. "Johnny, there's a man from your bank branch here with some papers for you to sign."

I excused myself asking the two agents if there was anything else that they needed from me. Darren said there was not anything now, but that they may have to contact me again if additional questions should surface. Darren handed him a business card and asked me to call him if I remembered anything else about the person they had discussed. I told them I would.

After the men left, Carla told me that she had lied and there was not a man from my bank at the front door. Carla had heard one of the men say he was with the FBI and saw the anxiety building in me, so she decided to insert a break in the Q&A session. I thanked her and said "they were asking a lot of questions about some guy named 'Guido' something, or 'Gilbert Kiefer'. Some guy who was at Stephanie and Derek's wedding reception, and was near me when I was talking to two other guys. I couldn't help them with any information. Maybe I should have given them Derek's or Stephanie's phone numbers. Oh, well, I'll give the FBI guy a phone call in a couple days with that information."

Carla and I went back to the groups of friends and family in the living room and family room.

The following day was just as forecasted: blue skies, a few puffy white clouds, sunshine and mild temperatures. The dedication ceremony for the Montgomery & Eloise Walker Children's Medical Center was grand and lengthy. Every person seemed to have long speeches prepared, except for the Walkers. They simply said that they were fortunate to have had a life good enough to be able to share what they have with children who are in need. A very prestigious part of the ceremony was reserved for the state governor to present 'Great Humanitarian Awards' to the Walkers for funding the new hospital wings.

Afterwards, a lunch was served under a huge tent set up on the open lawn area between the two main hospitals. All of the Walker family members were present including Dr. Gerald Walker, his wife Gerri and children, Derek and Stephanie Hunter, Carl and Carla, Andrea and husband Andrew, and son Andrew and his wife Agnes. Members of the state legislature, Mr. Walker's country club, and many members of the medical profession were also in attendance, including the new Pediatric Medical Chief of Staff Dr. Helen Eldon and her husband Dr. Milton Eldon, PHD. It seemed like a 'Who's Who' of prominent New England society and medical people.

It was just before the serving of lunch that I was talking with Carla, and her brother-in-law, Derek Hunter about the events of the day. Dr. Helen Eldon walked past the group and was immediately recognized by Derek.

"Pardon me," Derek said to her, "but I believe we have met before, somewhere. I recognized you, but I'm not certain from where."

"You have recovered very well from your collision with the front of a building in downtown Manhattan a long time ago. Do you remember me giving you some medical attention on the sidewalk?" Dr. Eldon asked.

"Of course I do," Derek said. "You're skills and gentle touch saved whatever features of my face that appeal to my wife. How nice to see you again." Derek replied. Derek then introduced the doctor to Carla, and I, whom she already knew from some personal banking transactions. I commented to the doctor that I was working with a realtor fellow with the last name of Eldon, and wondered if he was any relation.

"If you're referring to Jerome, or Jerry, the answer is yes. Jerry is my oldest son and lives here in Bridgeport. He and his family, being local, is another reason for me accepting the hospital's offer to be Chief of Staff for the new children's hospital. My husband and I get to see our son and his family much more often now. Plus, the change from the craziness and commotion of New York City to the slower pace of Bridgeport is much better for our health."

The group then discussed how grand the new children's hospital wings are and how happy the community is to have Dr. Eldon heading up the medical staff. She thanked them all for their kindness in welcoming her and her husband to the community and gave a personal 'thanks' to me for making their financial transition very painless and easy. She was just about to ask Derek about his next novel when a young woman approached her.

"Hi, Dr. Eldon, I'm Janice Wilkins from CNN news, can I speak with you for a few minutes? It's in regards to the new children's hospital and how you see it benefitting the families of this area." The young woman was tall, well manicured, and nicely dressed in a conservative business suit. She smiled at Carla, Derek and me, as I looked at her with a question on my face.

"Wilkins?" I asked. "I had a fraternity brother in school named Wilkins. Howard Wilkins. Any relation?"

"Why, yes. Howard Wilkins is my husband," She replied.

Derek laughed at that and said, "you're joking. Your husband doesn't happen to be in real estate, does he? Because a Howard Wilkins helped my wife, Stephanie and I, purchase our house in Westport. Couldn't be the same person, could it?"

With that, Janice Wilkins laughed and said that she believes the world to be getting smaller all the time, and this incident may just prove her right. "I know of that house. I also know of the stories being told about that house, and, I hope, someday, we can have lunch and talk about your house. There is some history there, and I have been researching the tales and wild stories associated with it. I would love to do a feature on your house and all that supposedly has gone on there over the years. Can we plan on that?"

"Of course we can," said Derek, "but now you really have piqued my curiosity about the place."

Before they could discuss Derek's house any more, Dr. Eldon received a page and had to excuse herself to answer it. She asked Janice Wilkins to walk with her so that they could talk.

While the children ran and played tag, the medical people grouped together and talked about new medical procedures, newest discoveries in their respective fields, and how nice the new Children's Hospital is equipped. Other groups talked about the market's ups and downs, while others talked about the weather. Everyone seemed to have a good time, in spite of the many speeches being given.

The event started to break up late in the afternoon with large groups of people leaving after thanking the Walkers, again, for their getting the hospital funded and built.

Derek and Stephanie looked around the grounds trying to locate Janice Wilkins to set up a day and time that they could get together. Stephanie saw Janice off in a corner of the grass area talking to two men in dark suits and wearing very dark sunglasses. At first glance Stephanie thought them to be Secret Service men, but did not believe any one of that level of importance to still be at the event. Stephanie and Derek decided to wait and contact Janice Wilkins another time rather than interrupt their conversation. Naturally, they both were curious about what Janice knew about their house, but finding out could wait.

As Janice Wilkins finished talking with Dr. Eldon, she received a call on her cell phone. Walking down stairs to the lawn area, she was talking with the TV producer that phoned her as two big men in dark suits approached her. She stopped talking to her producer and asked the men if she could help them.

Having identified themselves as being with the NSA and FBI bureaus, FBI agent Darren Miller showed a picture to Janice Wilkins. The man was somewhat strange looking, but not someone that Janice knew. Asked if she had ever seen this man before, she shook her head 'no'. She had a very good memory for faces, but could not remember having seen this person before. Janice, of course, asked why they were asking her about this man. Darren Miller said that they were involved in an ongoing investigation and could not answer her questions. He then showed her another picture of the same man with different clothes on coming down the jetway at an airport. Again, she said 'no' that she did not know the man, but did recognize the man behind him as Singman Lee, a Chinese importer/exporter who had been investigated by NSA for 'suspected' theft of vital U.S. documents from NASA's Houston facility. She looked at Darren and asked if the two men knew each other.

Darren shook his head and shrugged his shoulders saying "we don't know if they do, or not. We're simply trying to gather information on both of them. Thank you very much, Mrs. Wilkins. If you think of anything regarding either man, please call us immediately." He then handed Janice his business card.

Janice said she would and turned to walk away, looking for Derek and Stephanie Hunter who had already left.

Mr. & Mrs. Walker had rented the banquet room at the Brooklawn Country Club for a 'small' family dinner after the dedication festivities ended. The Walkers are not members, but their country club has reciprocal arrangements with other clubs across the country. The evening was shorter than most Walker family gatherings due to the length and activity of the day already. The children were slowing down from their day of running and playing, and the older family members were simply 'running out of gas'.

Mr. Walker did use the opportunity of all the family being together, to announce that they had sold the estate in Huntington. He said that he and Mrs. Walker were staying with Derek and Stephanie in Westport while a smaller, but more appropriate sized house, was being constructed on a corner of their property. He went on to say that he had retired from the financial firm he had helped to found, and would only be continuing with them as a board member. He thought that it was time for he and Mrs. Walker to relax more, and possibly learn to sail Derek's "Stephanie's Joy." He told everyone that all this would be starting right away and that both he, and Mrs. Walker are very excited about this phase of their lives.

The news from Mr. Walker was met with both applause and enthusiasm. All the Walker children congratulated their parents and expressed their happiness for them being closer to the rest of their family. Stephanie and Derek were thanked by her siblings for allowing all this to happen on their property. Stephanie explained that they had an entire third floor that was not being used and was perfect for her parents for their short term use once some minor remodeling was finished. In the meantime, Mr. & Mrs. Walker were taking a trans-Atlantic cruise from New York to London, and staying with friends in London for a few weeks. Both Stephanie and Derek thought it to be a 'win-win' situation.

I asked my sister-in-law, Stephanie Hunter, about a comment that the CNN reporter had made. "What are these stories that Janice Wilkins was referring to concerning your house? Sounded sort of strange, the way she phrased it."

Stephanie thought for a few seconds before saying "we're not entirely sure. We have heard stories, well, actually more like rumors, that the house was haunted. Some sort of sinister event happened there many years ago which, supposedly, wiped out an entire family. We started hearing these tales AFTER we bought the house and had moved in. Some people at the yacht club have hinted that it was a mass murder which killed all family members, but refuse to give any details. Very strange, but very, very unsubstantiated so far. We tried to contact the sellers realtor, David Jessup, but he has not been available, and his realty office is closed and locked." Stephanie leaned closer to me before continuing. "We have had some very strange 'happenings' start recently, and have no way of determining their cause. Things like a horrendous dead-meat-like smell, which seems to emanate from everywhere, and nowhere. A low groaning sound that cannot be found. A loud, no, very loud, crashing sound which shows no signs of anything having fallen. And some other equally strange happenings, none of which can be proven to have actually happened."

"Wow!" I said. "With all of that going on, why do you and Derek continue to live there?"

"It doesn't happen often, and it doesn't happen all the time. And, I'm not sure if Derek even hears it, or not. Maybe it's just me. Maybe I'm the only one who is experiencing these things." Stephanie answered. "I'm using some of the resources at my firm to investigate things and see what we can find out; both on the 'events' that are happening, and on the sinister event involving a family many years ago."

I simply looked at Stephanie for several seconds before asking, "does anyone else in the family know about this, or these events?"

Stephanie told me that they had not said anything to anyone, other than Mr. And Mrs. Walker when discussions first started about them moving in for a short time. Stephanie and Derek hardly even said anything to each other, and that I was now the only other person, other than the Walkers, to know about what they were experiencing. I told her I would keep everything she had told me to myself and not say anything to any other family member.

The days following the dedication ceremony and the Walker family dinner were pretty routine with everyone having gone their separate ways.

I was contacted by Jerry Eldon, the commercial realtor that Carl Walker, and I, had met with, and discussed purchasing property for the new branch location. Jerry told me that the property owners would make a 'better, and lower cost-per-square-foot' offer on a fifteen year lease, but would not be willing to sell the property. I listened intently, making numerous notes about the property, and told Jerry that I would convey the information to my boss in the City. I also thanked Jerry for his help with this property, but added, that this would most likely be the last time we spoke to each other. I knew my employer was adamant about buying, not leasing and they had other sites to consider.

I sent an email to Carl Walker with all the details of the new lease proposal I had gotten from Jerry Eldon. I felt certain that I would get instructions to contact the agent for another property we were considering.

It only took about a half hour before Carl Walker was on the phone asking me to get in touch with the realtor handling the second choice property and see what they could do. This property needed much more work done to it, as it had never housed any financial firms of any type. A complete interior 'make over' would be needed, but it was in a good location and was worth the effort and cost.

I first called Jerry Eldon and left a message for him telling him that we would not be considering any further lease offers and would be purchasing a different property. I thanked him for his work on this property, and said 'good bye.'

After touring the second choice location, and sending many photos to Carl Walker, I set up an appointment with the realtor for he and Carl to meet at the property with their contractor who did all their 'TI' work for the bank. The appointment was set up for Friday morning and Carl asked if he and Carla could 'crash' at my house for the weekend. "Of course you can," I answered, "the guest room is ready and waiting for you guys. Plus I would enjoy the company."

# CHAPTER 10

The Friday morning meeting with the other realtor went well, and the walk through showed a property with more square feet, and a few other advantages than the previous property. The bank's contractor found very few 'problems' with the building, and those that were found were very minor. The contractor gave Carl a 'ballpark' estimate on cost to bring the building up to CitiBank's standards, and some additional options, and said he would prepare a formal proposal when they completed purchase.

Carl and I discussed with the realtor price-per-square-foot for properties in the area and a deal was finally struck. The bank would purchase the site at a slightly under-market price with an option for an additional adjoining property on the south side. The additional property would be developed into a parking lot first, with future expansion of the bank's building being a consideration. Carl said that he would have their legal department draw up the papers and their realty division would handle the transactions and send the realtor all paperwork within a week. Carl wanted to complete the purchase as quickly as was possible and get the interior remodeling going so that they would be moved in and completely functioning before Fall arrived. And, because the seller was a customer of CitiBank, all financial transactions would simply be transfers between the bank's accounts and the seller's.

During a conference call between Carl, me, and the bank's directors in the City, we outlined the purchase price for the property, and an estimate for interior remodeling. Everyone agreed that it was a good deal and to move forward. Carl was given instructions as to whom to contact in their legal department to have the papers drawn up, and then to follow up with their real estate division people.

Carl wished everyone a good weekend, and said that he was staying in Bridgeport until Monday sometime.

Being in a celebratory mood, Carl suggested they order in some Mexican food and relax at my house with that and copious margaritas. I agreed and asked about Carla's status.

"She's coming in from the West Coast where she has been attending some research meetings at ChemCor. Her plane landed at Tweed-New Haven

Airport, and she's taking the Metro train from New Haven to here. So, if I can impose upon you to drive me to the train station when she calls, we can pick her up and then get our food. This way, she will not miss out."

I said I would be happy to, and suggested they stop by the branch to let my assistant manager know so he could close tonight.

Carla's flight was only twenty minutes late in landing, and she was on the Metro immediately thereafter. Carl told her what they planned for dinner and she said that sounded 'great' to her. She had been doing lunches and dinners at the research center meetings all week and would love to just kick off her shoes and drink margaritas. Maybe even get a little tipsy, she added. I grabbed her suitcase off the platform, and headed off for Mexican food and libations.

Mr. & Mrs. Walker stopped by the Victorian house on their way into New York City where they would stay in a hotel close to the cruise ship terminal. They wanted to check on the progress of the minor remodeling job before they left. Mrs. Walker had some very strong feelings about the new master bathroom that would be created and the décor that she had approved for it. Mr. Walker's concerns were simple: the shower flowed hot water, and the toilet flushed properly.

When the Walkers arrived, they discovered a stranger peering through the windows into the dining room area. Mr. Walker asked the man if he could help him in some way, which seemed to startle the man. Stuttering profusely, he said that he had been knocking on the front door for a long time, but no one answered. He was looking for 'odd jobs' and just wanted to see if anyone was home. Mr. Walker told him that he was in luck, if his son-in-law was not home, because he owned a big shotgun and was the type to shot first, and ask questions later.

The stranger said he was sorry and turned to walk off down the road when a police car pulled into the driveway. The police were just on regular patrol duty but saw something they felt was out of place when they started to drive by.

Seeing the police car, the stranger turned and ran in the opposite direction toward the river. Both police officers gave chase after the man, but he eluded them and vanished. "Probably jumped into the river and swam off," said one officer.

Mr. & Mrs. Walker identified themselves, and proved they belonged there by producing a key to the front door, and unlocking it. Mr. Walker explained their relationship to Derek and Stephanie, and the fact that they would be living there while the construction went on for their new house over on the far corner of the property. One officer seemed to know about this, and asked to go into the house, first, and check to see if it was empty and okay. Mr. Walker noticed that the boat slip for "Stephanie's Joy" was empty, which meant that they were out sailing somewhere.

Having done their inspection, the officers made their report about the stranger and left. Mr. & Mrs. Walker dropped off their boxes that they had brought with them, got Mrs. Walker's approval on the new master bathroom upstairs, and made sure everything was locked up and secure before leaving for the City. After New York City, next stop was London.

The delivery service delivered the food and Carl showed off his mastery of mixology for margaritas. The evening was full of laughter, margaritas, story telling, and some occasional Mexican food. Mostly margaritas.

Carla asked me if I had done any more investigating into the 'Keeper of the Keys' puzzle that they had been trying to solve on their last visit. I told her that I had not, because of work demands, Billy's medical condition, and a multitude of other things. I said that I had talked to Kyle Norton's wife and that she had confirmed that the key on the chain was the one that Sally had been so protective of. I had not seen anything else in Sally's belongings that would shed any additional light on what we knew already. Carl asked if I had gone through everything of Sally's, and I acknowledged that I had. I had put all of Sally's belongings into boxes in the garage and put the boxes overhead in the rafters.

"Wait, a minute!" I exclaimed. "Thinking about those boxes being in the rafters of the garage just reminded me that we put some of Sally's stuff up in the attic when we bought this house. I later had a contractor install the fold-down stairway so that she could get up there to it easily. I've forgotten all about whatever is up there; I've only been up there once and that was to change a light bulb for Sally."

By now both Carl and Carla were beginning to feel a little light headed from the margaritas that we had been drinking all evening, and the thought of having to climb stairs up into the attic did not sound too good. Carla suggested that we wait until morning and then we would have more light to see whatever was up there. I agreed and said that I was heading off to bed. Carla and Carl had already made their decision and followed me out of the family room to their guest room.

The following morning saw the three of us nursing pounding heads, bulging eyes, and drinking coffee and tea like it was water. The previous night's food was good, and the margaritas were even better.

Carla asked me if I wanted to have breakfast first, or go climb some stairs up to the attic. Carl voted for more coffee and quiet, but I said that I wanted to see what was in the attic first.

Off went Carla and I to pull down the attic stairs and make our ascent. Carl still needing more coffee, stayed in the kitchen and thought about the layout for the new bank offices.

I found the light switch and turned on the single light bulb so that we would not bump into anything and could see what we find, if anything. Suddenly the entire attic was flooded with light from several bulbs, and a half dozen fluorescent units which I was surprised to see. "Wow," I said, "there's a lot more light up here than I ever remember there was. I don't think those fluorescent lights were up here the last time I was. Wonder who installed them and when."

Carla was busy looking around at all the boxes, and other items stored there. In addition to the seven or eight cardboard boxes, there were two huge 'steamer' type trunks, four big suitcases, and three metal trunks much like you would find in a military unit.

I looked at all the items, also, and told Carla that this was much more than Sally and I had ever brought up here, and I had no idea whose belongings they are, or who carried all of it up here.

I lifted some of the cardboard boxes off the stack and set them down on the floor examining the writing on each one. They all seemed to have Sally's writing on them but did not say what the contents are. One box was marked "Photos" was heavier than the others even though it was smaller.

Carl decided to join Carla and me in the attic and marveled at how clean the whole area was, especially since no one has been up here in quite some time.

"Find anything?" Carl asked. "Whew! Thought you said there were only a couple of boxes up here, Johnny."

"Last time I was up here, there were only two large boxes, and two small ones. Looks like those boxes have gotten busy and multiplied," I said. "I don't recognize any of these other things. Wish I had thought to bring up a knife or pair of scissors with me."

Without hesitation, Carl whipped out a long switchblade knife and pushed the button on the top while watching my reaction as I stepped back a step. The blade shimmered in the bright light as Carl handed it to me to use in opening the taped tops of the boxes. I looked at Carl, a senior VP with an international financial institution, with one eyebrow raised and wondered to myself why he would be carrying such a weapon. While I cut the sealing tape of each cardboard box, Carla started going through the contents of each one, and Carl tried to figure out the locks on each of the trunks.

One trunk had a combination lock consisting of five numeric dials, each dial going from 0 to 40. Another had three separate locks on it with each lock requiring a key to open it. The final large steamer trunk had one single lock on it which somewhat resembled an old style door lock with the single key hole in the lower part of the lock. They all were different, and all very strange in appearances.

"By the way, Johnny," Carl said, "while you two were up here you got a call from a detective with the Bridgeport PD. He left his phone number and asked you to call him this afternoon after two o'clock. Said he was out of his office until then. I asked him if I could tell you what it was in regards to, and he said 'No', that you would know. I put the phone number next to the kitchen phone for you."

"Thank you," I replied, "he is one of the police officers investigating the car crash that Sally and the kids were involved in. He probably just needs to ask me more questions for which I have no answers. I'll give him a call back later. Thanks."

"If you need a good lawyer, don't forget about Stephanie," Carl said, "she's family and would not be cheap, but, would be billed at a family discount.

By the way, Stephanie phoned just before the police fellow did and asked if it was okay for her and Derek to stop by this afternoon. I called out to you but you must not have heard me. I told her that it would be okay. Maybe, if you have questions about this police investigation, you could ask her then. I hope that's okay."

"Yeh, that's fine." I replied. "My door is always open to family and friends.

Carla was not finding anything of interest other than clothes and items that the kids had made for Sally over the years. Even a broken ashtray that our eight year old son had made for her in day care when he was three. Mementos of days gone by, and of children gone away.

Carla found an envelope at the bottom of the second box and went through it. The envelope contained some very old sepia tone photos of people attired in very fashionable clothes for the time. It is a photo showing a family as if they were going to Sunday church services. Some photos of individual family members and some photos of an old Victorian styled house. Another photo showed the same house in the background, and in the foreground stood a husband, wife, four small children who were all dressed alike. Also shown somewhat in the background was a sail boat and three small children whose appearance led Carla to believe that they were someone else's children. Carla could not find anything, or anyone that she recognized in any of the photos.

I was not having any better luck with the bigger boxes I was going through. Out of style clothes, used baby clothes, and a small metal box at the bottom of one box was all I came across. I found copies of land purchases and recordings of title for various pieces of equipment, a boat, and a purchased item listed as a 'horseless carriage'. Then I found something interesting: faded copies of 'Certificate of Live Birth;' seven of them. One was not readable at all and looked to be dated from sometime in 1864. Another was dated from July 1897 and recorded the birth of one 'Jeremiah Keeper', son of someone and 'Thadeus Keeper'. Another was unreadable and also dated from sometime in the 1890's, and the rest were much more recent and easier to read. As I was trying to decipher all of the documents, my stomach started growling loudly. I looked at Carl, and Carla, and they both started laughing.

"How 'bout we grab all these documents and take them down to the kitchen for a closer look. Then we can get some breakfast going, also." I said to Carl and Carla.

We all picked up as many documents as we could carry and made our way down the fold-away stairs to the kitchen, and to the preparing of breakfast. It was only about a half hour later that Stephanie and Derek arrived at the house.

"Hi, guys!" Derek said as he entered the family room from the living room. His wife, Stephanie, was following closely behind carrying a briefcase in one hand.

"How is everyone doing this morning?" asked Stephanie. "Is that bacon I smell cooking?"

"WAS cooking," said Carla, "but two hungry guys finished off the last of it and Johnny doesn't have any more. He does, however, have more hash brown potatoes, eggs, and sausages, if either of you are hungry."

"Thanks, but no thanks, Carla." Derek said as he sat down on a chair. "Actually, we have eaten already. We were up early this morning and out of our house. Seems like we have a problem with the Victorian and we can't figure what is causing it, so we have a home inspection company going through it from the 'widow's walk' down to the basement. The contractor is also finishing the remodeling on the third floor suites for the Walkers. There wasn't much to do but we did have to develop a new kitchen, another bathroom, and a larger office for Mr. Walker. We, on the other hand, are on our way up the road to New Haven. I have an appointment there tomorrow with the Board of Trustees of the University of New Haven. Seems they need a professor of English Lit and they would like me to fill the position. I'm really not interested, but a couple of the Board members are old friends, well, actually Fraternity brothers of mine. So, I thought we would take a drive up there and listen. Good time while the house is being check out for the problem."

"What sort of problem?" Johnny asked.

"Just a whole lot of really weird things like a horrid, rotten-meat smell coming from somewhere, a loud noise that happens without warning, or cause. A growling-like sound that we can't find the origin of."

I looked at Derek before saying, "those are more than 'normal' type problems, wouldn't you say?"

Derek chuckled and said, "yeah, we couldn't get regular old termites, or cockroaches to handle. We had to go a step, or two, beyond that. We have to get everything taken care of before Mr. And Mrs. Walker are ready to move in."

"You two want some coffee, or tea?" Carla asked.

Both Derek and Stephanie agreed that tea would be great and Stephanie went into the kitchen with Carla to help prepare it.

"Since we got one of those 'Keurig' machines, we have really enjoyed afternoon tea together", said Derek. "Stephanie says it is so easy, even a husband can use it. One pod, one cup."

It wasn't more than a few minutes later that they heard Stephanie say "What is this?"

Stephanie stood holding two of the old documents that Carla and the men had brought down from the attic. "Where did you get this old picture of our Victorian?"

"What is all of this stuff?" Stephanie asked as she went through the stacks of old documents laying on the kitchen counter. "Why so many pictures of our house?"

"Are you sure it's your house, Stephanie. There are many Victorians around, and these are really old pictures." Carla said.

"Of course, I'm sure. Look at this eagle and half moon vent under the Widow walk. That was designed and made by the architect who originally designed, and built the house. That is a one-of-a-kind thing. No one else has that on their Victorian. Where did all this come from?" Stephanie asked.

By now, the men had come into the kitchen to see what the commotion was all about. Derek asked Stephanie what was wrong as he saw the very surprised expression on her face. She handed him several pages of the documents she was holding and told him "look at these."

Derek perused the various pages and held one for a long time looking at it. He took another from the pile he held and looked at it for a long time, also.

"These are both copies of pictures of our house; our house taken long, long ago and with other people in this picture. Where did you get all of these?" Derek asked.

I explained that the three of us have been up in my attic looking through boxes of stuff that Sally had put up there long ago when we first moved in. Along with Sally's old clothes, and objects from the kid's, were a bunch of documents and miscellaneous papers that we were just starting to examine in the kitchen's better lighting.

"But why would you have pictures, or rather why would Sally have pictures, of our house? I don't understand." Stephanie asked. "Are all these documents dealing with our house?"

I told her that we didn't know. We decided to bring the bunch of papers down with us, have some breakfast, and continue trying to put all the pieces of this puzzle together down here where we may be able to see better details on each document. I said that there were more documents in one box upstairs in the attic, but I did not know what they are.

"Okay, everyone," Derek started to say as he glanced at Stephanie before continuing on. "It's time that we come clean with you guys regarding our Victorian. I apologize for lying to you before, but we have had one hell of a time lately with a situation that sounds too bazaar, too unreal to really be true. Stephanie and I hardly believe it, ourselves. I don't know if you remember a fellow named Guido Kiefer, or not. He was one of my groomsmen at our wedding. Well, it seems Mr. Kiefer, whose real name is Gilbert Keeper, was assisting the top two people at Sorrabon Publishing steal millions of dollars and was also selling corporate information to the Chinese. He had been involved in politics on a state level here in Connecticut, and had several foreign and American contacts with which to deal." Derek paused to examine everyone's facial expressions before continuing.

"Guido, or Gilbert, had been a friend from college that I had kept in touch with over the years, and looked to be headed to the Connecticut Governor's office when something went awry. The NSA has investigated him for his involvement with the Chinese, and the FBI has been investigating Gilbert because he and his 3 siblings are believed to have some sort of evidence regarding the identity of the murderer of their entire family. A murder, which, by the way, happened in the living room of our Victorian."

Carla asked Derek and Stephanie if they wanted to sit down and have something stronger than tea or coffee.

Stephanie thanked Carla and said that they may have 'something' a bit later. Then she started telling the group about the night several weeks ago when Guido sneaked into the house, waited until she and Derek came home from a dinner out, drugged her, knocking her unconscious and tying both her and Derek up and binding them to kitchen chairs. He threatened to kill them several times and was in some kind of frenzy looking for something he thought was hidden in the house; something that his father had hidden and he wanted it. He demanded it because he thought it was his.

"Thankfully," said Derek, "the FBI guys, and Stephanie's lead investigator, had been shadowing Guido for some time waiting for him to make a move; and, he did. He also severely damaged almost every interior wall in our house, not to mention tearing down the ceiling in several rooms. This includes all our remodeling that's being done to the third floor for Mr. & Mrs. Walker. Just very, very thankful that they are in the U.K. This could have been horrendous had they moved in already. So, it is the repairs that are actually going on right now, and not some 'home inspection'. We will be witnesses in his trial next week and the prosecution expects that he will be sent away for the balance of his life; just on the Federal charges. Then there are the state charges which can be filed and he can be tried on for those." Derek paused a moment to take a sip of his cold tea.

"My God!" said Carl giving his sister Stephanie a big hug. "I had no idea that you two had gone through such an ordeal. Why didn't you say something before now?"

"The FBI was very strict about what we could do, where we could go, and what, if anything, we could say about any of this," Stephanie said, "we had to know that none of his siblings were shadowing Guido's movements and would come after us to finish what he had started. Both the NSA and FBI fellows think that Guido was working alone, without assistance from his brother, or sisters, and we are 'somewhat safe' now."

"Does the FBI know where Guido's brother or his sisters are at?" asked Carla.

"Not at this time," answered Derek. "Guido stayed local and changed his name and appearance, but his brother and two sisters have probably scattered to the four corners of the country, changed their names and everything else about them."

"The head FBI agent on the case thinks that one of the sisters may still be in this area somewhere under a different ID," said Stephanie.

"Wait a minute!" I said very loudly. "That name...the last name that I've been hearing you two say...was it 'Keeper'? I ask because one of these documents has that as a last name for someone."

Carla asked me if I was sure that was the name I saw, and I said that I am. With that, everyone took some of the documents in their hands and started to thumb through them, page-by-page.

"Right here!" said Carla. "Look at this. A copy of a 'birth certificate' for one 'Jeremiah Keeper'! Here is another one for a 'Thomas Allan Keeper', and a third one for a 'Sally Ann Keeper'. There may be more of these in those documents." Carla picked up another pile of papers to look through. Many of the documents were so faded and old that they were unreadable, but some gave clues as to who these people were.

The group spent the next hour and fifteen minutes going through each and every page that they had, setting the pages that were readable off to one side, while putting those that would not give any information at all in another stack.

I was staring at one single page for several minutes when Stephanie asked me "why would Sally have all these documents stored away in your attic. Why would she care about any of these people, especially Gilbert Keeper?"

With that question ringing in my ears, I put the page I had been examining down and said, "perhaps, just perhaps, because her last name had been 'Keeper'? This birth certificate is for 'Sally Ann Keeper' and is about the same date as MY Sally's birthdate. When we got married, she could not find her birth certificate, so we had to get another from a hospital. But it was not a certified copy, so we had to get a doctors sworn statement as to her birth and citizenship. That statement, if I remember right, was signed by the doctor who is now at our children's hospital. Dr. Helen Eldon."

Everyone looked at each other in amazement. Could any of this be true? Could my severely injured wife actually have been a part of a family being sought by the FBI?

"Aren't we being a bit crazy here?" asked Carl. "I think we are all really, really reaching on some of these points to try to link something together. We've all known Sally for many years and we all know her to be a truly loving mother, wife and friend. How do you now connect her to this 'Keeper family' thing, and, especially Gilbert Keeper?"

"Maybe this would help," said Stephanie holding up an old black and white photo of a family on some type of outing. Someone had written on the back of the photo, the names of each person pictured. Pictured along with three adults were children of varying ages. One child was identified as 'Gilbert Keeper', another as 'Helen Louisa Jessup', another as 'Thomas Allan', and still another as 'Michael J. Fowler'. A baby being held by a female in the picture was identified as 'Sally Ann Keeper.' The baby looked to be about six to eight months old and the date on the picture would make it to be about the time that Sally

Hamilton was born. This just led to more confusion among the group, and everyone seemed to have had their breath knocked out of them.

"I'm almost afraid to ask what else is in those boxes," said Stephanie. "Does anyone know?"

"We haven't finished going through the rest of the boxes, nor have we opened the suitcases, the three big trunks, or the three metal trunks which are somewhat smaller in size," said Carla. "We took time out to eat breakfast, and that's where we were at when you arrived."

"Well, I, for one, believe we have a huge puzzle here that involves things which we don't know much about," said Derek. "If it's all right with you, Johnny, maybe all of us should go up there and dig into things more. No telling what more we may find; or nothing else. Who knows?"

I agreed.

Just then the doorbell rang and I got up to go see who it was.

Derek could see me talking to someone as if I knew the person well. I just sort of hung onto the front door and leaning into a friendly conversation. After a minute, I stepped aside and a large man with a gold police badge hooked onto his belt stepped into the living room. He followed me through the living room and out to the kitchen where everyone else was gathered.

"Everyone, this is police detective Brian Simpson. He is with the Bridgeport Police Department, and is investigating the collision that took place between Sally and the pickup truck," I said. "He is now, also, looking into the collision that I had recently, and thinks that the two collisions may be linked in some way. He has some questions, so I invited him to ask all of us."

I then introduced each member of my family to the officer, one-by-one.

Detective Simpson told everyone about the department's investigation of the accidents, and how they were beginning to piece together facts that led them to believe that it may not have been an accident after all. He showed pictures of different men and asked if anyone knew any of them. All heads were shaking 'no' to every question. He then showed a final picture of a young man about mid-to-late twenties, and I said that this young man had been into my old bank a number of times asking questions about loans and such. I recognized him because he asked for me by name and while we talked, the young man was very nervous, would not make eye contact, and did not always make sense with what he was talking about.

Detective Simpson asked more questions about those meetings before showing another photo of the same young man. This photo had his beard shaved off and his hair cut short. No one reacted to the new look for the young man, so the detective put the photo back in his folder. Detective Simpson was just about to end his talk when he mentioned that it appeared to the police crime scene investigators that the young man may have driven the vehicle that struck and killed the boy on a bicycle, and then crashed into the van driven by Sally Hamilton. "Evidence found by the investigators showed his name was Aaron Franklin, and, as near as they could determine, he was living in a flat up by the university with another fellow named Don Jessup. This Don, or Donald, Jessup is some type of electrical genius who designs and builds very elaborate electrical contraptions. Jessup may have been involved, in ways still unknown, with Aaron Franklin, or with the vehicle Aaron was driving. At this time, we do not have enough answers to all our questions to state anything conclusive."

Stephanie looked at Derek and knew exactly what questions were bouncing around in Derek's head as she said, "excuse me, detective, but did you say his last name is 'Jessup?'"

"Yes, I did." Answered Detective Simpson. "Why? Do you know that name?"

"As a matter of fact," replied Stephanie, "we are going through documents and other stuff that Johnny has in his attic, which his wife had stored up there years ago when they moved into this house. One document is an old picture which showed a child identified as a 'Jessup' child."

"Plus," added Derek, "when we bought our house, the seller's realtor was named David Jessup. Is that only coincidence?"

"That wouldn't have been local, would it?" asked Detective Simpson. "David Jessup from Westport?"

"Yes, it was. He handled the seller's portion of the sale of our house, and worked out of an old, rather shabby office building in northwest Westport," added Derek. "I think I still have his contact information here on my phone, if you need it."

"No, thank you," replied Detective Simpson, "we know of David Jessup, and have been trying to locate him for several weeks. He appears to be the father of Donald Jessup, and is also known to the Federal authorities as somewhat of a radical 'anti everything' type person. His offices and his apartment upstairs from the offices, have both been deserted for quite some time. We obtained a Federal search warrant, in conjunction with the FBI, to search the property, but did not come up with anything that I can discuss regarding this incident. To date we have not been able to find either Jessup; David or Donald. If that picture is handy, can I see if for a moment?"

I could feel the hair on the back of my neck reacting to the detective's use of the term 'incident.' This was NO incident! This was manslaughter committed by a drunken driver; an action which killed two of my children, AND, it left my only remaining child, and my wife clinging to life in a hospital ICU for months and months.

Get a hold of yourself, I thought. The detective is only doing his job, and is trying to help solve this 'incident.'

Carla handed the photo over to Detective Simpson and asked if anyone wanted more coffee or tea. Detective Simpson studied the photo for several minutes, making several notes from it, before handing it back to Carla.

"Mr. Hamilton, you have my card, but I'll leave a few more here on the counter in case any one of you can think of anything additional. Or, if you discover any information in the documents that you're going through in your attic." Detective Simpson said as he laid some of his business cards on the kitchen counter.

After that, the detective thanked everyone for their time and cooperation and asked them to call him with anything they find. He reminded them that almost any little thing that they discover, can turn out to be the key item in this investigation. "Report anything!" he told them.

As I was showing the detective to the front door, Carla and Carl were staring at each other for a long time. Stephanie noticed this and finally asked Carl if there was something that he wanted to share with the others.

Carl laughed at Stephanie's question and said, "well, you know how some things or words stick in your mind? How a single word, a single move, or a single sound will bring to mind other things. It's a 'Pavlovian' type of thing; but when the detective said 'that almost any little thing that we discover, can turn out to be the key item in this investigation', it reminded both Carla and me about poems, and phrases that we, and Johnny keep coming across that use the word 'key'. As in "Key man", and "Keeper of the Keys". That's what the three of us were discussing a couple weeks ago, and how does it give any clue to what happened."

Stephanie continued looking at Carl for a few minutes before asking "well, did you come up with any answers? Or, just more questions?"

"Guess you would say just more questions." Replied Carl. "There is definitely some link between the word 'key' and what everyone is chasing, but we cannot figure out what."

"Maybe the answer is still within all the stuff we have to go through up in Johnny's attic." Carla said as she filled everyone's coffee cups.

"Maybe we need to concentrate on going through the rest of those documents and see what we find."

I heard this as I entered the kitchen and agreed, but did not want to rob everyone of their days off from work and other errands that they needed to do. I tried to explain how much I appreciated everyone's willingness to help me, but said that I felt guilty for robbing them of their free time.

"Bull shit!" exclaimed Carl. "Just plain bullshit! You aren't robbing anyone of anything! You're the one who got robbed; robbed of most of your family by this fellow driving under the influence. And, if there are more people responsible for this, besides him, than we all need to find out who they are, and bring them to justice. Besides, this is what family does; helps one another!"

With that, Stephanie shouted "group hug!" Everyone got up and joined in the hug with me in the center. After a few seconds, they all broke off the hug and headed for the attic stairs to begin their quest for more possible information.

I had already set up an appointment at the hospital with Dr. Eldon and a pediatric psychologist to meet and discuss Billy's further medical treatment. Carla convinced me that the rest of the group could handle things until I returned.

As I headed off to the hospital, everyone else headed up to the attic. "Wow," said Stephanie, "look at how sparkling clean this whole place is and all the bright lights to see things better. I thought this was going to be more like the attic in our Victorian: dusty, dirty, and full of hundreds of cobwebs. This is nice."

Derek agreed and asked Carl what they had accomplished while they were up here last time. Carl said that they had started to go through the boxes of things, and to open up the suitcases and the metal trunks. They also were examining the envelope of documents that had been found which they ended up taking downstairs to the kitchen to read. Two boxes had been gone through by Carla without finding anything of importance, or value. Derek asked if any of the suitcases or the trunks were opened, to which Carl replied 'no.' Derek had brought with him a hammer, pry bar and a couple big screwdrivers in case they needed to pry open any locks or things; it appeared they would. Derek looked closely at the lock on one of the huge steamer trunks and saw that it required three different keys to open each of three different locks on it. Another of the huge trunks had four numeric dials with numbers from 0 to 40. The final trunk had one single lock which was very large and required a specially shaped key to unlock it. Derek decided that the suitcases would be the easier items to tackle and he had the tools to do it. He and Carl lifted one suitcase up and put it on top of the stack of trunks and looked at the lock. Out of curiosity, Derek tried to open it and was amazed when the lock popped open without any force. He opened the top and found only women's old maternity clothes, along with some maternity items inside.

The men put the suitcase on the floor, off to the side, and picked up another suitcase. This one was not nearly as heavy and was also filled with women's clothes and some photos of more recent times; Johnny and the three kids were all dressed in costumes as if they were going to celebrate Halloween. Nothing else was of interest or value. They then grabbed another locked suitcase which would not open. Derek got the pry bar he had brought up with him, and started to pry open the stubborn locks. One lock popped right open with little effort by Derek, while the other required much more force and language. It finally popped open and Derek lifted the lid of the suitcase. There amidst clothes and baby shoes were photos of children running around on a dirt lot, possibly playing baseball, although no bats or gloves were visible. Other photos of children playing in a big open area of some sort, and, still, other photos of a family picnic. Also among the clothes and photos was a piece of paper with the following poem neatly printed in ink:

IN A HOUSE SO DARK AND COLD, THERE LIES A TREASURED TALE,

WHEREIN IS KNOWN THE BODIES COLD, THAT SENDS SOMEONE
   TO JAIL,

WHEREIN IS TOLD THE STORY BOLD, THAT TELLS OF YOU AND
   ME,

JUST ADD THE TIME THAT YOU WILL FIND, FROM THE KEEPER OF
   THE KEY.

Both Derek and Carl read the poem over and over before handing it to Stephanie to read. As Stephanie finished reading it, she simply looked at Derek, and then asked "what in the hell does this mean?" As that was being asked, Carla walked over and took the paper out of Stephanie's hand and read the poem. She read it a second time before looking at Carl and asking if he understood what it meant.

"No," Carl answered, "but I think we can decipher it and possibly discover what it means."

"Derek and I think we can shed some light on this," Stephanie said. "It may relate to the murder committed in our house some seventy or eighty years ago. A murder now referred to as the 'Keeper House Murders."

Derek chimed in "what if we assume that this poem, or even all the poems we find, refer to our house and the murders committed there. What if we do that, and see how much sense we can make from what we find."

As they all worked at going through the newspapers, clothes, children's items and a myriad of other types of things, no one noticed that over three and a half hours had passed since Johnny had gone to the hospital to see Dr. Eldon. Everyone was quickly reminded of the passing of time when Johnny called out to Carla from the bottom of the attic stairs.

"Up here, Johnny," Carla answered. "We're up here in the attic working away. We're making some headway if you want to come on up."

"Let me change clothes quickly and I'll be right up." I answered as I went off to my bedroom to change. "I have Dr. Eldon with me, Carla, can you come down and talk to her while I change. Thanks."

Carla looked at everyone else with a curious look on her face. No one could figure out why the doctor would come back from the hospital with Johnny, but all were certain that they would eventually find out why. In the meantime Carla climbed down the attic stairs and greeted the doctor who was sitting in the kitchen looking at the day's paper.

"Hi, Dr. Eldon," Carla said, "please excuse my dusty, casual appearance but we are going through some items that Johnny's wife, Sally, left stored up there. Boxes and boxes of kid's clothes, and  some items that the kids had made for her."

"Do you have children, Dr. Eldon?" Carla asked.

The doctor answered that she and her husband have two sons who are both grown men. One is married and lives here in the Bridgeport area with his wife and two children, and the other has started teaching at New York University, where her husband Milton teaches Philosophy. Having one son and his family living here was an added incentive for accepting the position of Head of Staff for the new children's hospital, the doctor admitted. Carla and the doctor discussed how the new hospital was functioning and the difficulties the doctor was having in finding enough qualified staff to staff every position properly. Dr. Eldon was describing how far west she had gone to locate doctors and nurses when I walked back into the kitchen. I was carrying several of Billy's favorite action figure toys, which the doctor was going to take back to the hospital for Billy. The doctor had discussed with me the possible benefits of having some of Billy's familiar toys with him to help with his recovery.

Dr. Eldon took the toys from me and said that she must be running along as she was on her way to see her son Jerry and his family.

I thanked Dr. Eldon for delivering Billy's toys to him as we were walking to the front door. The doctor said that she would be calling me in a couple days to set up appointments for me to work with the pediatric psychiatrist.

After the doctor left, I thanked Carla for talking with the doctor and keeping her company while I changed my clothes. Then I asked what they had found in the boxes.

"Come on up and we'll show you what we have been able to piece together." Carla told me as we both headed for the attic stairs.

Derek and Carl started showing me some of the various documents that they had found within the suitcases, while Stephanie laid out documents and notes that they have found within all the papers. Stephanie, having more experience with putting together bits and pieces of information in order to build lawsuits, or defense strategies, started talking about a sequence of events ranging from the approximate date of the murders, up to today.

Stephanie guessed that possibly the children that authorities thought had been killed by the murder(s), had actually escaped being killed. If that were the case, then they would have knowledge of who the murderer, or murderers, are, and how they got away; possibly even where they escaped to.

Stephanie also thought that within the papers that they had that there are clear, concise pointers to who the Keeper children are today, and what their professions are. Stephanie told me that there are "just too many clues, like the notes and the poems, that point to people who have survived the murders and have changed their names, and moved on with their lives. If the children did not commit the murders, than they certainly know who did. Maybe they are on the run trying to stay ahead of the murderer and to stay alive, themselves."

The question Stephanie could not answer was: if the Keeper children were not murdered, then who were the children that WERE murdered with the two adults? None of the information that they have found so far, points to any other children being around other than the four Keeper children.

Derek started talking about the various poems and notes they have found, and asked me if I knew any more about Sally's background than what they all knew. I said that I did not. I believed that Sally was an only child, raised by an aunt who had wealth and left Sally money when the aunt died. We met in college and Sally took a job with a local travel agency here in Bridgeport to help pay off her student loans after graduation. Sally and their next door neighbor, Kyle Norton, worked together at this travel agency until Sally got pregnant with our first child and she quit working. Derek asked me if I thought that Kyle would know any more about Sally's early years. I said "probably not", but that Kyle's wife and Sally were pretty close and that Kyle's wife had already told me some things about Sally that I didn't know before. Derek thought maybe they should invite Kyle and his wife over for dinner and talk to them both about what they may know.

I told the group that they had me over for a delicious dinner, so it would certainly be appropriate to reciprocate. I said that I would make that happen.

Suddenly, the air that had been coming into the attic seemed to disappear.

"Hey! What are you doing?" yelled Carla.

Just then, I saw the attic stairs being closed and secured from down below. I yelled out to whomever was down stairs, but received no response.

I asked Carla if she saw who closed the attic stairs, and Carla replied that she just caught a glimpse of a man; not someone she recognized. Maybe eastern European, or Latino male, but she couldn't be certain.

I yelled out, once again, to the person downstairs to stop joking around and release the stairs so that they would open. I listened for a minute or more but got no response. I could hear someone moving about in the hallway, but could not tell where he was going to, or what he was doing.

The more I moved and yelled out, and the more stressed everyone became, the hotter the environment became. Soon the men were perspiring profusely, and the temperature started to become very uncomfortable for all. It was then that I realized that someone had turned on the electric snow melt for our home's roof; an added luxury that I had installed several years ago when they had a similar system installed in our new driveway. This, however, was not winter time and all that the roof system was doing was to rapidly raise the temperature in the attic.

I asked who, among the group, had their cellphone with them. Derek had left his on the kitchen counter, Stephanie's was in her purse in the kitchen, and Carla's was on a nightstand in the guest bedroom being charged.

"I guess I win, then," said Carl, "I have mine and I'm trying to find a spot where I can get more than one 'bar' of signal strength."

I told Carl to never mind about signal strength, and to dial a number. I gave Carl the phone number of my next door neighbor, Kyle Norton. Carl dialed the number and listened to the phone ring, and ring. Finally, Kyle's answer machine picked up and Carl left a message that we were all stuck in my attic and to please come over and open the attic stairs. After ending the call, Carl dialed 911 to report a break in at my address and people being trapped in the attic. About half way through his call, Carl's phone went dead. He looked at the display and saw it was completely dark. He knew what Carla was about to say.

"That's exactly why I plug my phone into the charger every night: so that calls don't end in the middle. You should have charged it, Carl," said Carla.

Carl knew Carla was right, but he wasn't going to say a thing. Instead he took out his handkerchief to mop his face of perspiration. Just then the attic lights went out and the group was enveloped in complete, and utter, darkness.

"Not good!" exclaimed Derek, who suffered with nyctophobia and would soon become an absolute 'basket case.' Derek's fear of the dark has been treated by his doctor for many years, and, although he has gotten better, he is still sent into an extremely agitated mood.

"Not good, at all," Derek repeated. Stephanie knew that she would have to find Derek in the dark, somehow, and begin talking him into a state of calmness.

As Stephanie was trying to feel her way around the area and get to Derek, Carla asked if anyone else smelled gas.

At that moment, it became clear that whoever was down stairs, doing whatever they were doing, had intentionally turned on the gas in the kitchen.

As the odor of natural gas became stronger in the attic, Stephanie made her way to Derek and was talking to him in very low, comforting, words.

I knew we needed to break out of the attic quickly and turn off the gas in the kitchen before the house exploded into pieces. I asked Carl if he remembered how far away he was from the area of the attic that was without plywood flooring. Carl thought a minute before saying that he thought that he was, maybe, twenty to thirty feet away. I asked Carl to keep talking while I tried to find him in the dark. While Carl talked about nothing in particular, I felt my way around trying to locate where Carl was standing.

Finally I found Carl and was able to start to get my bearings on where in the attic we both were standing. Slowly I made my way away from Carl, only to trip and fall over one of the suitcases that had been set aside. Going straight down onto the plywood floor, I landed on my face and outstretched arms and hands. I let out a grunt when I landed hard, along with a swear word, or twelve.

Hearing the loud crashing sound above, the two policemen who had come into the living room to check on a report of an odor of gas, yelled out asking if someone was up there.

"Yes, we are," I answered. "We're up here in the attic, who ever you are. Please unlock the attic drop-down stairs in the hallway, and let us come down."

Moments later, a blinding flood of light came shooting up through the entrance to the attic along with a gush of cooler air. I led everyone down the stairs and into the 'welcome' of two Bridgeport Police officers with their guns drawn.

I tried to explain who we all are, and how we came to be trapped up in my attic. About this time, two workmen from the local gas company arrived to inspect the house's gas service and check all my gas appliances.

The police officers listened for a few minutes and then asked for identification from everyone to confirm what we were saying was true. It was then that I discovered that my wallet, car keys, cellphone, and cash were all missing. Same was true for Stephanie's purse and attaché case, and for Carl and Carla's cellphones and money.

Both Carl and Derek could provide ID's since they kept their wallets in their pants pockets when they first went up into the attic, but my ID was gone. As the officers took down what each person told them happened, Kyle Norton walked into the kitchen. Seeing the two policemen, Kyle excused himself and turned to leave.

"Wait, Kyle," I said, "these officers need confirmation that I am who I say I am. We were trapped up in the attic by someone; someone who stole all our personal property, and tried to do us in by turning on the gas."

Kyle showed his driver's license to the officers and confirmed that Johnny was the owner and resident of the house, and that the other people were who they said they are.

I finally asked one of the officers how they happened to be in my house. The officer said that the '911' line received an anonymous call reporting the odor of natural gas; possibly coming from this address. He said that they were half a block away checking on an abandoned auto and responded to the request for a unit to check out the report. They immediately confirmed the very strong odor of gas to the gas company and decided to check the property. They found all windows and doors closed tight, but the back door was unlocked. Upon entering they heard a loud crashing sound from up in the attic, and the rest everyone knew.

I, along with the rest of the group, gave the officers a list of personal property that was stolen. I told the officers that we would continue checking throughout the house and update the list, if additional items were found to be missing. Along with the missing money, car keys, et al, all of the documents that were on the kitchen counter were also gone. No one could understand why anyone would steal that type of stuff, but gone, they were.

The two officers finished their reports and bid everyone goodbye reminding me that I needed to stop all credit cards, and report the theft of my auto and license to the State Motor vehicle office right away.

After the officers left, Kyle asked me exactly what had happened. As I was relating our experiences to Kyle, I was reminded of the proposed dinner being planned with Kyle and his wife.

"Kyle, are you and your wife doing anything for dinner tonight?" Johnny asked. "Before all this happened, Carla had offered to prepare a big dinner for all of us tonight, and she asked about inviting you and your wife over. Any plans?"

"Actually, we are going out for dinner." Replied Kyle with a half smile on his face. "Out to our next door neighbor's house, that is. What can we bring?"

I turned to look at Carla, who was preparing water for tea for Stephanie and herself. Carla thought for a minute, and finally told Kyle that if he wanted to bring a bottle of red wine, that would be perfect.

With that, Kyle asked about the time for dinner and said that they would be back then. Carla and Stephanie headed off to the market for items that could not be found in my cupboards. In the meantime, I started calling my credit card companies, and making other necessary phone calls. My auto, and driver's license, would have to wait until Monday morning.

The dinner was fabulous. Carla and Stephanie and Derek prepared Italian food that was fit for the best chefs in Italy. The wine was paired perfectly with the food, the conversation was light and very often quite humorous, and it was, I thought, the most enjoyable and fun evening I had had in a long time.

Stephanie steered the conversation around to Sally and tried to get as much information from Kyle's wife as she could, but her answers were usually short and without details. Both Kyle and his wife seemed to want to stay away from the subject of Sally Hamilton. Finally, I decided to take charge of the questioning.

"Guys, we are finding lots of information regarding Sally that is both puzzling, and incomplete as regards her early years and extended family," I said. "We hoped that one of you might have some insight as to who she was, where she came from, and anything else that we do not have clear details about. But, let me say, that is not the reason for this dinner. My family needed a break from me and my questions without answers, and, I think, they all wanted to talk to people about some other subjects, and to be able to laugh a little."

I looked at both Kyle and his wife for a few seconds before continuing, "and, I'm sorry if these questions make you feel uncomfortable, or that you might feel that you're betraying a trust if you answer. It's simply that we have so many, many questions that do not have answers to, and we need help."

Kyle's wife sat quietly for a few minutes before she started telling me how sorry she was that she had not been more open and forthright with us before now. Again, she assumed that because Sally and I were husband and wife that I would have known all there was to know about her already. She asked me about the key and gold chain that they had discussed already.

"Oh, my God," I replied, "I had completely forgotten about that key. When I found it, and the gold chain, I was discovering an envelope of documents that I needed to go through. So I dropped the key and chain into the pocket of my shirt, and I haven't worn that shirt since. It must still be in the pocket."

With that, I went off to my bedroom closet to retrieve the key and chain while the group continued talking.

When I returned, I showed the key to Kyle's wife to confirm that it was the same key and chain that she had seen Sally wearing. She said it was and asked if anyone had figured out why Sally thought so highly of it that she would not let anyone else hold it. I guessed that that was just Sally being Sally.

Kyle asked what exactly we were looking for, and why the concern about Sally's past and her family. Stephanie, being accustomed to answering these type of questions without giving an answer, said that they were tracing ancestries, and when they inputted Sally's information, as they knew it to be, into the computer, that nothing would come up. It always showed incomplete ancestry.

Kyle looked at all the faces around the dinner table before saying, "okay. Fine, if you don't want to tell us what is going on, then we cannot help." He then looked at his watch before looking at his wife.

I knew at this point, that I would have to tell Kyle and his wife something; problem was, how much can I tell them, and how far can I trust them? I thought about those questions briefly before saying to Kyle, " we're being asked questions by the Police Department, and the FBI about Sally's accident, and other matters, and it's become embarrassing at times to not be able to answer the questions that they ask. We all decided that we needed to know more about Sally's early years and her family before the next question, or two, that we cannot answer."

Kyle looked at me and asked, "I can understand the police department asking questions, but why is the FBI involved in an auto collision accident? Seems like that's way out of their league."

"We don't know why the FBI is asking their questions," I said, "They just say 'it's an ongoing investigation' so they are not at liberty to discuss anything." I hesitated for a few seconds wondering whether or not I should continue before making the decision that I should. "The police do not think that the collision with Sally was an accident. They think there was something premeditated and planned about it, and involves others. Again, they are not giving many clues as to why they believe this, just asking a lot of questions."

Finally Kyle's wife looked at me and said how sorry she was that they had not been closer to Sally and I, and had been better neighbors. She said that Sally had told her once that she had a sister, and two brothers. She didn't know where they were, or anything much about them because they all had been separated by their parents at very early ages. She said that she felt she did not have a childhood, and was so happy that her children were going to have one.

I had been looking at the table top while listening, looked up at Kyle's wife making eye contact. "Guess Sally was wrong about that, wasn't she," I replied.

Carla, who had started to clear away dinner dishes, along with help from Stephanie, asked if it was time for coffee and tea, or was everyone still at the 'another sip of wine' stage. Seems the wine won out.

Kyle's wife asked me if I knew that Sally was born in Connecticut. I said that I did not; I was told that she was born in Ardmore, Pennsylvania; a very affluent suburb of Philadelphia, and that both of her parents had been killed in a plane crash while she was staying with an aunt.

It seems as though everyone who Sally confided in got a different version of some story. Carla believed the Connecticut story, though, because one of the pieces of Sally Ann Keeper's birth certificate that she was able to piece together showed birthplace as "New Haven, Connecticut." That much they had been able to determine to be true. There was still much more to decipher, and confirm. Kyle and his wife spent another hour, or, two additional glasses of wine, telling everyone at the table everything that the both of them knew about Sally. I did discover a couple new things about Sally, and her other family members; nothing really earth-shattering, just new.

Finally, Kyle thanked everyone for the dinner and nice evening, and said that he hoped that the two of them had been of some help with the ancestry endeavor. With that, Kyle and his wife bid everyone 'good night' and left.

After finishing with the loading of the dishwasher, and getting it started on its' task, Derek and Stephanie left to go to their hotel downtown. Derek had work to do on his current novel, and Stephanie had legal briefs which she had to go over. They said that they would be back in the morning, after breakfast, to resume helping with the attic.

Carl, Carla and I finished straightening up the family room and sat down to watch the evening news; seems the rest of the world insisted upon going on, even though the three of us did not have answers to all the world's problems.

# CHAPTER 11

After breakfast at the Duchess Family Restaurant, we all headed back to my house to resume our searching through the items in the attic. This time would be different, though, as Carl and I have installed an anti-locking device on the door mechanism for the fold-down stairs. No one was about to trap anyone in the attic this time.

My telephone was ringing as we walked into the house. I ran to answer the ringing phone too late; it went into voicemail. I stood near and listened to the message being left by Bridgeport Police Detective Brian Simpson about the police department arresting a man in my neighborhood who possessed some of my credit cards. The detective wanted me to phone him and set up a time when I could come into the police station and possibly identify the man. Since I had not really seen the person who closed the steps, I thought I'd better ask Carla to go with me.

Right now, though, our focus is to finish going through all the stuff in the attic and see if some sense could be made of the few clues that we had. Carl had come up with some sound ideas about the terms, which we discussed at breakfast.

I also wanted to see a document that they had left in the attic that referred to a 'Helen Louisa' something, and another with the name of 'Helen Louisa Jessup.' I thought they were one and the same person; problem was, who is this ONE person.

Carla commented on how much better she felt being in the attic and knowing that we could not be trapped there, again. The anti-locking device gave all a sense of calm this time.

With everyone working feverishly to sort through papers, pictures, and such, I noticed the trunk that Derek had mentioned earlier with the peculiar lock on it. The more that I looked at it, the more it looked familiar. Then it came to me, and I said "hold on a minute! I think I have one solution in my pocket." With that I took the gold chain and key out of my pocket and walked over to the large trunk. I put the key into the lock and it fit; it fit perfectly and with the slightest of turns it unlocked the trunk.

I looked up at everyone's surprised faces and smiled. Slowly I opened the top of the big steamer truck to find it full of clocks; clocks of every size and color, every description packed into the trunk.

Carl guessed that there were probably 150 to 200 various clocks, most of which were the old-style 'alarm' type clocks with the winding key and manual alarm set on the back of the case.

As we all stood amazed, looking down at the trunk full of clocks, Stephanie asked why there are four clocks of the same size, color, and style laying face up on top of all other clocks. I looked at Carl, who looked at Derek who sort of shrugged his shoulders. Then Stephanie asked about one of the poems that we all had read, and how it said something about "add the time..." Stephanie asked if that was really what it said, and if yes, then look at the four clocks. Going from the left side to the right, the clocks read: 12:00, 10:10, 3:15, and 1:35. While Stephanie was talking, Carla was finding the paper with the poem written on it. Carla read the poem aloud:

"IN A HOUSE SO DARK AND COLD THERE LIES A TREASURED TALE, WHEREIN IS KNOWN THE BODIES COLD, THAT SENDS SOMEONE TO JAIL. WHEREIN IS TOLD THE STORY BOLD, THAT TELLS OF YOU AND ME, JUST ADD THE TIME THAT YOU WILL FIND, FROM THE KEEPER OF THE KEY."

Carla confirmed it! Stephanie was correct about adding the time together, but now the question was: add it together for WHAT?

Carl asked how would someone add time together? How can you add twelve o'clock and get something other than twelve o'clock? Derek said that "maybe that IS the answer. Maybe the first number IS 12."

Stephanie asked what the number would be for, which has everyone scratching their heads. Then Derek said that in one of his novels, he had clocks on the wall tell a combination to a lock that would set his hero free from imprisonment. Carl looked at everyone and said, "we have four clocks, which can give us four numbers, and we have a trunk here with four combination locks on it, which prevent it from being opened. Why not try the numbers on the locks?"

Everyone agreed and Carl turned the first combination lock to 12 and watched as it popped open. Derek then told Carl to turn the second lock to 20. Carl did and the second lock popped open. Derek said the third number, by adding 3:15 together, would be 18. Carl turned the third lock to 18 and it opened right up. Derek said that 1:35 would be the number 36. Carl tried 36 on the fourth lock and it, too, opened right up. Now the trunk, which once was held closed by four locks, was completely ready to be opened and its' contents examined.

I walked over to the big trunk and reached down to raise the top up, when, suddenly, gunshots rang out, and the sound of bullets piercing stucco and wood could be heard. Everyone fell to the floor and Carla and Stephanie tried to crawl behind the trunks for shelter. All the rest of us simply stayed as flat on the attic floor as we could get. The gunshots continued to ring out and pierce the walls of the attic at random. I could hear men yelling outside but could not hear exactly what they were saying. Some bullets came through the attic floor from below, fortunately missing everyone's sprawled bodies. The yelling filled in between the barrage of gunshots which seemed to come every fifteen to twenty seconds for many, many minutes.

Finally, someone with a bullhorn was yelling for "anyone up there; up there in this attic, come down immediately with arms in the air and your hands behind your head. Come down NOW!" the voice yelled.

I yelled back that I am the homeowner and I'm not doing anything until I know who is telling me to. "Identify yourself, and do it now!" I said.

"This is special agent Rogers with the FBI and I have a SWAT team with their guns trained on the ceiling. You have ten seconds to come down before I give the order to start shooting. Now, come down with arms raised and hands clasped behind your head. How many people are up there?"

"I am Johnny Hamilton. This is my home and property and I am up here with four relatives, agent Rogers. I will do as you ask and then let the others know if you are telling the truth, or not. Then they can decide to come down, or not." With that, I inched my way to the drop-down stairs and started the descent down the ladder.

As I reached the bottom, someone grabbed me and put handcuffs on me. I turned around to see about ten men, all dressed in total black combat uniforms and pointing very large, menacing-looking, guns at me.

I asked who agent Rogers is. The tall man standing nearest me, identified himself as special agent Rogers and showed me his ID and badge. I read his identification fully before yelling out to the others that it is okay to come on down with arms raised, as instructed.

One, by one, Carla, Carl, Derek and Stephanie made their way down the attic stairs and into the arms of waiting FBI agents. As each of my family members reached the hallway floor, they were placed into handcuffs.

Agent Rogers sent two other agents up the stairs to check the attic to see if it was really empty. Getting a confirming "clear" for their inspection of the attic, agent Rogers asked what we were doing in the attic.

Stephanie identified herself as an attorney, and demanded to know why we all had been put in handcuffs without being given our 'Miranda Rights."

Agent Rogers smiled and said "Ma'am, if you really are an attorney, you know we have the right to restrain a suspect before we have to give that person their 'Miranda'. Now let us conduct our business without any of you saying anything that would jeopardize your legal rights." Agent Rogers gave directions to his men and let them conduct searches throughout my house. I watched them as they fanned out into all the rooms looking for someone, or something. Finally, I decided to press my luck as I asked agent Rogers if he had a search warrant that he could show me for what was going on. He laughed and began giving each one of us our rights under the "Miranda Act."

Agent Rogers then asked which one of us is Cecil Oldham. We all just looked at each other as Stephanie asked who Cecil Oldham is, and why was there so much shooting going on. I told agent Rogers my name again, as did Carl and Carla Walker. Stephanie and Derek did not say anything, yet, waiting to get an answer from the agent.

Agent Rogers seemed to be getting annoyed at us because none of us was the person he was looking for: Cecil Oldham. "It will do you no good to hide behind an alias, because I know that Cecil Oldham is in this house. Now, which one of you is him?", asked the agent. When none of us confessed to being this Cecil Oldham person, agent Rogers told his men to start tearing the walls apart, and for a couple men to tear the attic apart looking for it.

Stephanie yelled at them to stop; not to tear anything apart and to remove everyone's handcuffs immediately. Stephanie informed agent Rogers that she had placed a phone call to her office and that the entire time, everything that was occurring was being listened to and recorded by 12 to 15 attorneys, and because agent Rogers had not properly given them their "Miranda's", and had not produced a court issued search warrant that agent Rogers and his entire group of agents were in violation of federal laws. Now Stephanie just stood and glared at agent Rogers waiting for his next move. Agent Rogers seemed to be thinking about what Stephanie had said, as well as his possible next move, and told his men to "stand down" for a moment. He then walked over to stand almost nose-to-nose with Stephanie and ask "and, where would that cell phone be hidden, Ma'am? Do I have to search for it?" Agent Rogers took a step backwards and started a very slow, almost lecherous and lustful, look up and down Stephanie's body while showing a small smile on his lips.

"And where do I start my search, Ma'am?" Rogers asked. "Where would you hide a cell phone?"

As agent Rogers raised his hands to begin unbuttoning Stephanie's blouse, Stephanie tried to take a step backwards but was prevented from doing so by another agent. Rogers unbuttoned the top button of Stephanie's blouse and started to reach for the belt on her jeans when a loud voice came from behind everyone, "stand down, Rogers! Stand down and back off, NOW!"

There in the family room doorway stood FBI agent Darren Miller, and the NSA agent Devon Miller. "Stand down! Back off! And take a break out in the sunshine. Go walk it off, Agent Rogers! NOW!"

FBI agent Miller stood about three inches taller than agent Rogers, who, himself, was a tall, imposing figure of a man at over six feet tall. When agent Miller spoke, every FBI agent seemed to know that his was a voice of authority and paid close attention. Agent Rogers seemed to weigh his options, in his head, before moving through the group of agents and walking out the back door into the bright sun outside.

Agent Miller instructed the other agents that everyone was to have their 'cuffs' removed, and that he can vouch for everyone. He apologized to all of us and made a special apology to Stephanie. "I completely understand if you want to file a complaint against agent Rogers, and these other agents. Here is my card with the local office phone number on it and they can help with forms and such, if you so choose. I'm very sorry that this turned out this way. We were engaged with several men whom we have been shadowing for some time. These men apparently want someone, or something, they thought to be in this house, Mr. Hamilton, and were about to enter with guns drawn. Agent Rogers saw the pending danger and called for backup agents. When the additional agents arrived, two of the men drew their firearms and pointed them at the agents, and that started a fire fight that led to the deaths of three of the four men. Agent Rogers thought that more of that group might be inside this house, and acted accordingly. I believe he may have gone a step, or two, too far, but he was trying to end the confrontation and determine if any other accomplices were in the house."

Stephanie stood listening to agent Miller while she rubbed her wrists to alleviate the pain caused by the handcuffs. "Well, that's all very interesting, Agent Miller, but that fact is that these agents, for whatever reason, brought an action and search without a court issued search warrant, and that, sir, is illegal," Stephanie said. "Improper 'Miranda rights' and illegal searching will not be ignored, and that's before the indecent search that I had to endure." Stephanie reached inside her blouse and retrieved her iPhone and held it up to her ear. "Forrester, did you hear everything that went on?" asked Stephanie to someone on the phone, "and everything was recorded? Good. We'll make copies for backup and safety and I'll review it when I'm next in the office. Thank you for your help and to everyone else there. Have a good day." Stephanie ended the call, and put the phone in her jean's pocket. "Mr. Miller, we will review everything and make our determination later. Right now, we need to get on with higher priority matters. Is there anything else that you need from any of us?"

"We will need someone to look at the deceased bodies and tell us if any one of them is recognized and can be identified. Then we need identification of the remaining, live person whom we are detaining in our van outside. We will be taking that person to Boston to undergo interrogation as to what this group was up to." Agent Miller replied.

We all looked at each other several seconds before I spoke up, "I don't know that looking at dead bodies is a like, or a specialty, of any one of us. Do you think that these deceased men are locals and that's why you want us to look at them?"

"We don't know. They may be locals, they may be from the west coast, we do not know, but if you, or any one of you has seen one of them before, maybe at a gas station, maybe at a circle K store, it gives us a starting point to begin our investigation," Agent Miller said. "Mr. Hamilton, with you being a bank manager, I had hopes that you may have seen one, or all, of them sometime before"

I thought for a moment before saying "I understand Agent Miller, and I'll be happy to take a look; but no guarantees."

With that, we all went outside to an absolute flurry of activity; photographers taking pictures of walls of my house, empty shell casings on the ground, the whole driveway area, as well as the entire back yard. Many other people were placing small orange cones on the ground next to empty shell casings, others were covering the dead bodies after photos were taken from every angle possible. Still others were taking measurements from some points on the property, to other points on the property. And, among all the activity, there on a small fold-up type chair, sat agent Rogers simply watching everything being done and not doing anything, himself. Agent Rogers now looked like a whipped puppy as he sat with his hands folded in his lap, and his armor and gun belt off, and his FBI sunglasses gone. He watched each agent do their thing and never said anything, nor lent a hand to anyone.

Stephanie, Carla and Derek held back away from the rest of us as we walked across the back yard to where the first dead body laid. You could tell on their faces that they had no interest or desire in viewing the bodies. I had to agree with the three of them in the desire department, but felt some sort of duty since this occurred at my house. Why, suddenly, were all these really bad events happening at my house? Was I now under some sort of curse that all bad events would happen at Johnny Hamilton's house? Or, happen to Johnny Hamilton?

As an FBI agent pulled back the top of a body bag to expose a dead body, I tried to be as analytical as I could, but, was really enthralled by the very strange coloring in this dead person's body. Light gray mixed with light rose coloring was interrupted by occasional blotches of pale flesh tones. Here and there could be seen deeper, darker shades of blue and purple, but no where were there any deep, dark blood red colored spots. It was as if this fellow died but did not bleed.

Agent Miller had been talking to me for several seconds without me realizing it. "...do you?" agent Miller was asking. "Do you recognize this fellow, Mr. Hamilton?"

"Sorry, Agent Miller, I do not." I answered as I looked at Carl who was shaking his head 'no'.

The agent covered the body, again, and we moved to the second body bag, which another agent was pulling back the top cover. Another interesting palette of mixed colors for skin, but I did not know him. This fellow appeared to be much younger than the first fellow had been; maybe early twenties. Much too young to have had his life ended already. Then I had a flashback to my five year old son, Billy who was being kept alive by medical machines. Steady, Johnny, I thought. Steady, and stay focused on what you're doing.

As we moved over to the third body bag, Carla suddenly said, "this was the delivery boy, and looks like the guy who shut us in the attic!" She was standing looking at the still uncovered, body of the second gunman. I looked at her and asked, "are you sure, Carla? You said you didn't get a good look at him before he closed the attic door. How can you be certain, now?"

Carla walked toward us and said, "that heart tattoo on his neck on the right side, I remember seeing that just as he closed the attic door. And, he is the fellow that delivered our Mexican food the one night that we ordered in, and drank too, too many margaritas. He delivered the food. Don't you remember, Carl?"

Carl moved back to the dead body and studied it for a few minutes before saying, "Johnny I think Carla is right. He is the delivery guy from the Mexican restaurant. I remember I was fumbling with my money trying to come up with an exact amount and give him a decent tip, so I only looked at him at the last minute. That is him."

Agent Miller was busy making notes of what was being said between us, and asked Carl what the name of the Mexican restaurant was. Carl replied that he did not know because I had placed the order and he had simply answered the door. I was busy thinking of which restaurant I had ordered from that night and finally remembered. I gave the name and location to agent Miller as another agent lifted off the cover on the third dead body.

"Wow," I said. "This guy I have seen before. Give me a minute, or two, and let's see if I can remember where." I tried to recall the time and place, but could not. I know I have seen him but the rest of the picture is not as clear. As I walked around the body, again focusing on the mixture of grays, purples, blues, and such in his skin coloring, I suddenly remembered.

I looked at agent Miller, who was standing there looking right into my eyes, and said, "this fellow came into my bank, that is my Citibank branch, with Tom Kitchen, when Tom came in to talk about small business loans for his various businesses here in town. This guy and Tom were busy talking until they entered the branch, then

Tom came over to see me, and this guy went to talk with my senior teller. He was there for maybe 20 to 30 minutes and then left before Tom did."

"And, this Tom Kitchen fellow," agent Miller asked, "he is a regular customer of the bank? You said he owns businesses here in Bridgeport?"

"Yes," I answered, "Tom owns the clock and jewelry store, the electronics store on the north side of town, and the Ace Hardware store just a couple miles from here."

Agent Miller was busily making notes before calling a couple agents over to huddle with him. After a few minutes, the other two agents took a slip of paper from agent Miller and turned and left. Agent Miller looked back at me and asked, "how long have you known this Tom Kitchen fellow?" I explained that Tom had been servicing Sally's grandfather clock for several years, by her request, but that I had only met him when I took over the local Citibank branch. Tom came in one morning to introduce himself and get more information about small business loans. Before that, I had only talked to him on the phone.

"Let's take a look at this last fellow and see if you know him, shall we?" agent Miller said to Carl,

Carla and I as we walked toward the FBI's operations van. As we got to the rear doors, it was obvious that a wrestling match, or a fight of some sort, was going on inside the van. Agent Miller opened the partially closed doors and asked "what in the hell is going on in here?" He turned and quickly apologized to Carla for his language, but she said there was nothing to apologize for.

It seems that the fourth suspect, whose hands were cuffed and behind him while he sat on a built-in bench along one side of the van, had somehow gotten his hands in front of his body and had nearly stolen an agent's gun while the agent was completing paperwork online. It took several men, and a female agent, to get the suspect back under control.

Agent Miller assisted everyone to upright the suspect, sit him back on the bench, and handcuff him to an overhead rail so that he could not duplicate his feat again. When he was upright and looking at us, Carla said that she had seen him before; a time or two around town. Carla remembered him from the hospital and the dedication of the children's hospital wings. She said she was pretty certain that he had had on hospital scrubs when she saw him there.

While all the activity was going on in the driveway, and the back yard, no one had noticed two men slipping into Johnny's house through the front door and being inside for several minutes. All the agents, and everyone else were focused on what was happening, and what had happened in the back of the house, the side driveway and back yard. It was not until Dr. Chambers arrived in the back yard that anyone was even aware of these 'other people.' Dr. Chambers saw them leaving Johnny's house and getting into a van parked out front as he was parking his car on the street out front.

Agent Miller and several FBI agents ran out to the front immediately but everyone was long gone. They searched up and down the residential streets but did not find any sign of the van.

When agent Miller returned, he immediately asked Dr. Chambers if he had gotten a license plate number, to which the doctor replied "no." Dr. Chambers did not suspect that anything was wrong until he was walking up to Johnny's front door and found this picture, and piece of newspaper laying on the front porch.

Dr. Chambers handed both to me and asked what had happened. I looked at both items before handing them to Carl and Carla to look at. The picture was a photo of one Sally Ann Keeper at a high school prom, and pictured in the photo with her was a young man identified as a Cecil Oldham. The picture identified the high school as "Wilbur Cross High School", a very large school in New Haven. The newspaper was a part of an old New Haven Register front page where the lead story was a review of the 'infamous' murder of the entire Keeper family in Westport.

I looked at Dr. Chambers and asked him why he was here. Dr. Chambers said that he had been trying to phone me all afternoon, but kept getting a message saying "the number you have dialed is no longer in service, or you have dialed the number incorrectly." Having heard that message some ten to twelve times, Dr. Chambers decided that he had better drive by and check on me.

Agent Miller walked around the corner of the house and after a few minutes told me "it appears,

Mr. Hamilton, that a couple stray bullets went through the telephone connection box and severed the phone lines. Not one chance in a million that this could happen, but it did! Twice. I'll call the phone company and get someone out here right away."

I looked at Dr. Chambers, again, and asked "why were you trying to phone me all afternoon? What happened?"

It was at this point that Dr. Chambers glanced at Carla, and Carl before answering my question. He looked at his shoes, and then said, "it's your son, Billy. He had a double cerebral hemorrhage during the night and didn't make it through the emergency operation. I'm so very sorry, Johnny, we did everything humanly possible to save that young man, but his hemorrhaging was just too severe." Dr. Chambers stood staring at me.

"He's dead?" I asked. "He's dead...gone?" I couldn't believe what I was hearing. I couldn't believe that this was all true; that today had really occurred. This must be some sort of cruel, torture that only a devil could dream up. It must not be real! "Really?" I asked. "Really dead?"

"I am so very, very sorry," Dr. Chambers said as he stood looking at Carla, who had tears forming in her eyes.

I collapsed onto the grass and simply sat and looked at the ground. I couldn't look anyone in the eye; could not utter a single word, and could not believe that what the doctor was saying was true. Carla came over to me and put her arms around me to comfort me, but all I could do was to stare. Finally, after five to six minutes, I looked at Carla with tears in my eyes and told her that I didn't know what to do. "I don't know if I can continue on," I told her, "I don't know if there is a reason to continue on."

Stephanie and Derek, who had sensed that something terrible was happening, came over to where Carl, Carla and I were sitting and asked what had happened. Dr. Chambers told them about Billy's death and how it happened. Stephanie started crying and had to be comforted by her husband. Everyone was emotionally invested in my five year old's battle for life, his battle that was now lost. Death one. Billy zero.

Finally, Stephanie asked Dr. Chambers if Sally's condition had changed any. He told her and

Derek that she was 'technically dead' and only being kept alive by machines. Dr. Chambers told them that this was another bridge that would have to be crossed soon: whether, or not, to continue keeping her alive and on life support. Derek said he did not think that this was an appropriate time for that discussion, and the doctor agreed.

After everyone had composed themselves and were able to stand up, again, agent Miller asked me if it would be possible to do a walk-thru my house and see what, if anything, the mystery men may have stolen. I looked at him, knowing that he had been very patient with us while we digested the news about Billy, and said "of course." I asked Carla to go with me to help determine if the mystery fellows had actually stolen anything, or not.

We walked back into the back of the house while agent Miller and two armed agents followed. Carla and I did a step-by-step, foot-by-foot walk through of each and every room and found nothing missing. Agent Miller even asked us to open all drawers and cabinet doors and check inside. We still found nothing missing. We were beyond confused as to why two men would sneak into my house and do whatever they did.

"Wait a minute!" Carla exclaimed. "The items that the doctor found out front were not from your things; they were more likely from Sally's things. Like the things in the attic. Let's go check the attic!"

With that, all five of us went and climbed the stairs up into the attic space. There, where we had been busy at work much earlier, sat the big steamer trunk with its' lid wide open and all but a couple shreds of paper gone.

Agent Miller looked into the empty trunk and asked me what was in it before. I told him that I did not know because the five of us were working up here to solve puzzles and clues that would allow us to open it, and the other trunks. We had just gotten the final lock off the trunk, and were about to open it up when the shooting started. At that moment, we all hit the floor and tried to stay away from flying bullets. We never got to see inside the trunk until now.

After looking around the attic and making notes about the damage done by bullets in my attic, agent Miller and his two other agents went down the stairs and outside to their van.

Carl called up to Carla and I that the rest of the group was in the kitchen making coffee and tea. Carla looked at me, gave me a big kiss on my cheek, and said that she was going down for a cup of tea, and, maybe some bourbon.

# CHAPTER 12

Billy's funeral was much smaller in size than the one for my other son, and daughter. We were able to hold this one in the funeral home, and have many of his school friends, and his friends from his 'T-ball' team attend. Once again, my family, especially Carl and Carla, helped me beyond words with everything. I was in somewhat better shape than previously, but still I was a 'basket case'.

Mr. & Mrs. Walker came back early from England, having gotten the news from Stephanie of everything that was going on here in Bridgeport. Mr. Walker talked to me like a father would, and really helped me to be strong through the ceremony. While he has not lost any of his children yet, he and Mrs. Walker did lose two still-born children, and Mr. Walker lost two brothers during the war. Something about listening to him talk made me feel a little better.

The Walkers hosted a dinner after Billy's funeral was over at the Brooklawn Country Club here in Bridgeport. It was mostly family with the addition of Dr. Helen Eldon, and her husband, Dr. Chambers, and his wife Sonya, and a small handful of other guests. The dinner atmosphere was more solemn than other family dinners had been, maybe because this one was following the funeral of a five year old.

After almost everyone had left, I thanked Mr. & Mrs. Walker for coming back home early and attending Billy's funeral. I especially thanked Mr. Walker for being there for me and for his words of strength and encouragement. As they were leaving, Mrs. Walker gave me a big hug, a kiss on my cheek and whispered in my ear to remain strong; she said that her family needs me. Mr. Walker had asked me earlier in the evening, if I had made any decision regarding Sally. I told him that I had not, but I knew that one must be made pretty soon. He told me that if I ever wanted to talk about it, just phone him and he would meet me.

For a man like me, whose parents were killed during his senior year of undergrad school, it means a lot to have a Mr. & Mrs. Walker in my life.

I returned to the bank branch, and to my daily routines with mixed emotions; sorrow for the way my family has been effected by one driver's actions, and excitement about how well the banking part of my life is going. The branch has been growing in number of deposits, personal loans, and commercial loans. Carl Walker has asked me to open branches in four other cities in the New England region and has approved my recommendations for locations.

But, in all of this was still my unanswered question about what to do about my wife, Sally. How do I take the chance, or probability, of ending her life by removing her from the life support equipment. How do I know if I am doing the right thing, or not? I am still wrestling with having to make that decision. I am still unable to talk with Dr. Chambers and answer his question about Sally. I have read, and heard, about people who were in deep comas for months, and month, and awoke one day to resume their normal lives. It has happened, why can't it happen now? Why not Sally? I need someone close to me; I need someone who knows the answers to all my questions about gold chains, and keys, and pictures, and everything else we have found.

I returned from a 'road trip' on a Friday afternoon, after attending the opening of our new branch in Providence, RI. We opened this branch shortly after enlarging our small branch in Worchester, MA, and opening a new branch in

Springfield. I opened the Springfield branch just half a block, and across the street, from the Royal Bank branch location which is managed by Sumner Adams.

During the grand opening, Sumner came by to check out our facility, and to catch up on things that have happened to both of us since I left Royal Bank. Sumner and his wife have separated with her returning to Atlanta to be close to her family. Sumner was obviously saddened by that event, and was also quite vocal (off the record, of course) about the poor management of Royal Bank. He was not as certain that he made the correct career choice now as he was when he and I parted company. Before he left the branch, Sumner asked me (off the record again) to keep him in mind should I hear of any really good openings within the financial world; he was quietly looking to leave Royal Bank without jeopardizing his job. I told Sumner that I would keep that information very confidential, and keep him in mind. With what information Sumner was willing to share with me at that moment, I had a much better understanding of how Royal Bank was conducting their day-to-day banking business.

I was fortunate to have hired, and trained, a very good assistant manager for my Bridgeport branch, because without him I would not be able to do all the regional branch business that Citibank was asking of me. I was even more fortunate to have appointed this fellow's sister as my new manager for the new Springfield branch. This was something, the positioning of a female branch manager, that had some of the 'old school' males scratching their heads in amazement.

After phoning the branch, and getting updated on everything that has happened since I went on the road to Rhode Island and Massachusetts, I decided to change clothes and relax before getting some 'take out' for dinner. Amazing that our house, which had been a warm, loving home for our family, seemed to take on the personality of a dark, foreboding structure without any soul. It had no laughter, it contained no love, it never again enjoys the sound of children's giggles. It still was cool, in the hot weather, and warm in the colder weather, but it did not seem welcoming to me whenever I returned to it.

I listened to the 8 or 9 voice mail messages on the answer machine, making notes to return calls to family members and business colleagues. I always had to smile to myself when there was a voice mail from my sister Carla. She had enough humor in each message to make me happy to be home; even if home was no longer the old, happy place it once was.

I had changed clothes, and was trying to decide between Chinese and Italian take out dinner when the front door doorbell rang out. I opened the door to find Detective Brian Simpson standing there with another police officer.

"Good evening, Detective Simpson," I said. "To what do I owe this pleasure?"

Detective Simpson introduced the other officer and told me that the Bridgeport Police Department had made several arrests recently, and would like me to come to the police station tomorrow for a lineup to see if I could identify any of the suspects arrested. I asked what time and said that I would be there. I asked Detective Simpson if I should bring anyone with me, like an attorney, or relative who may be able to identify people. He said that I may be asked to do that at a later date depending upon how this session goes.

I thanked Detective Simpson and said I would be there tomorrow.

After the policemen left, I got back to making choices; choices between Chinese and Italian. But, before I left to pick up some dinner, I felt I had better give Stephanie a phone call and advise her of what is happening. With an attorney in the family, so to speak, it is always wise to get good legal advice.

My phone call to Stephanie went directly to her voice mail. I did not want to leave a message about something so trivial, but I did want her input on this matter. I left a message and grabbed my car keys; keys to my new car sitting in my driveway. Since the collision with the 'self-driving' vehicle some time back, my insurance company decided to write off my older auto as a complete loss. With the money that they gave me, some savings dollars, and a small bonus from Citicorp, I purchased a new car. A car that would hold up to the numerous 'road trips' I would be making in my capacity as New England Regional Vice President for Citibank.

I was just leaving the Italian restaurant with my take out dinner when my cell phone began ringing. I could tell from the ring tone that it was Stephanie returning my call.

Taking the phone out of my pants pocket, I said hello to Stephanie and asked her to hold on a minute as I got into my car. Once inside my car I tried to explain my purpose in calling in 25 words or less. Stephanie asked me if the police detective said anything that made me suspicious, to which I said 'no.' Stephanie said that she did not do 'criminal law', but that her firm had a very large department that did, and if I needed advice tomorrow while at the police station, just phone her and she would dispatch someone. She also advised me to not say anything other than the bare minimum of words. I thanked Stephanie and asked her how Derek was doing on his latest novel. She replied that his 'management duties' running the Sorrabon Publishing operation has begun to hamper his writing time. Worse than that, he has virtually no time for researching any ideas that he gets for a new novel. Stephanie said that even the 'yachting time' is suffering. I asked if there is anything I could do to help, to which Stephanie thanked me and said no. She said that Derek would just have to learn to manage his time better.

I arrived at the police station early and met with detective Simpson and a uniformed officer to discuss how today's process would go. Detective Simpson said that FBI agents would also be in the room because much of what the Bridgeport PD was investigating was now becoming a Federal case, too.

After a few minutes of Detective Simpson's reassuring me that none of the suspects can see me to identify me, we walked down to the viewing room.

The room is about eight feet wide and maybe fifteen feet long with one entire wall solid 'one-way-viewing' glass. This glass wall separates our room from another room about the same size; except the other room has the far wall marked off with lines and numbers every six inches to show the height of each person. The room has three other Bridgeport police uniform officers and Agent Miller from the FBI already talking among themselves when Detective Simpson and I walk in.

After introductions to the rest of the officers, our room goes dark and the entire other room is made very bright with high-intensity floodlights. It was only two or three minutes later that a line of men were marched into the other room and given instructions to stand on the marks on the floor, with their backs against the wall. It was clear to me that the men could not see us where we are, and judging by their actions they were acting as if they were looking into a mirror on their side.

One-by-one, each man was made to turn around by doing a series of right turns. After the last of the eight men had finished, Detective Simpson asked me if I recognized any of the men. Looking at all of them, studying their features for a long time, I told the detective that I had seen number two, number five and number seven previously. Every head in the room turned to look at me after that statement. Detective Simpson had one eyebrow raised when he asked me, "are you certain? Numbers two, five, and seven?"

I continued looking at the eight men staring back at me in the adjoining room and said, "yes! Number two is a customer of my bank and is in my branch periodically. Number five, I believe, is a member of the Bridgeport PD and I've seen him in his uniform, and number seven I have seen in my neighborhood three or four times, but do not know if he lives there, or not." I turned my head and looked at Detective Simpson with a slight smile on my lips. The detective just stood there for a few seconds looking at me without saying anything. He then turned and pushed an intercom button on the wall near him and told the policemen in the other room "okay, take them all back and hold them."

"Mr. Hamilton," the detective started saying, "you have correctly identified Reverend Thomas of the Church of Christ who works with our police department as a volunteer. You are correct, he is a customer of your bank. The second man is police sergeant Mike McCoy of our Bridgeport PD, and the third man is Kevin Kitchen. Now his is a name that you should recognize...do you?"

"I know a Tom Kitchen," I replied. "Any relation?"

Well, apparently Kevin is an adopted son of Tom Kitchen, according to detective Simpson, and he and two other men were in possession of photos, copies of birth certificates and other papers which apparently came from my house. "There is also a great deal of additional information which pertains to your sister-in-law Stephanie and her husband. The Feds want to have a meeting with everyone at one time, but you say that your sister is out of town? When will she return?"

"I'm not sure," I answered, "but I believe she will be back this coming weekend. I can call her husband and find out for certain if you want."

Detective Simpson said that would not be necessary, that next week will be fine.

At this point agent Miller of the FBI said that his bureau needs to have everyone meet at the same time to discuss information that various law enforcement agencies have uncovered regarding my wife, my family, and various other members of my extended family. Agent Miller said that the FBI office would be in contact with everyone involved and set a day and time for a meeting. He then thanked me for coming in and participating in the lineup procedure.

I asked agent Miller for more information about Kevin Kitchen, but he said that everything that the bureau knows will be discussed at next week's meeting. He thanked me again, said he would see me next week and he and several other men left the room.

# CHAPTER 13

Monday morning started off with a conference call between several regional vice presidents and the Manhattan main office management for updating personnel data. The company needs to fill more branch level positions, as well as looking at opening four new branch locations. The conference call lasted nearly ninety minutes and gave me the opportunity to give Sumner Adams name and experience to my bosses for their consideration. Seems some of our people know of Sumner, by reputation, and would like to set up a meeting with him. I said I would make the initial contact and arrange a telephone meeting with Sumner.

The FBI made contact with all of the family members involved, and a meeting has been scheduled for Thursday afternoon at the Bridgeport police department headquarters. Mr. & Mrs. Walker will be attending even though they are not directly involved in the findings by the FBI. I asked agent Miller, during a phone conversation, what new topics would we be discussing at this meeting, and he simply said that "everyone will be brought up to date with the various investigations being conducted, and what each law enforcement agency knows…and how it effects each member of the family."

I have promoted my assistant branch manager to full branch manager in order to give me more time to conduct the business of the bank on a regional basis. It was something I really enjoyed doing, and I believe I gave the other employees some positive reinforcement that they too can rise above whatever level they are currently at. I love to promote from within and my bosses gave me the 'green light' to do so. Now, with my 'new' used car, I would be on the road going from branch to branch much more often. This is a part of banking that is new to me, and I welcome the opportunity to learn all about it. Carl Walker anticipated that I would be moving up soon when he designed the new offices for our new building. He proposed a large office, much larger than I thought necessary, with many perks built in for me so that I can come and go without getting caught up in the branch's flow of business and customers.

I talked to Sumner Adams regarding our bank's plans for expansion, and Sumner told me that he was definitely interested in talking with management. I asked Sumner to mail me his resume to my home address, I would review it and pass it on up the ladder. Sumner actually sounded excited about the possibility because things were continuing to spiral downward at Royal Bank.

Thursday arrived rather quickly and came with dark clouds and light rain. It seemed appropriate for this afternoon's meeting at the police department. Later today, after the meeting with the 'Feds" concerning their various investigations, I have a meeting with Dr. Chambers at the hospital regarding Sally and her condition, and future health. Yes, the rain seemed very appropriate; add dark of night, heavier downpour of rain, vicious lightning and thunder, and things would be perfect.

The meeting room that is being used in the police department building is the same room where the morning roll call is held. A very unassuming room void of color, void of decorations, simply a functional room with tables and chairs. Both agent Miller of the FBI, and special agent Miller of NSA were at the front of the room arranging their respective notes and getting ready to start the meeting.

I looked around the room and saw my family members were all seated and watching the two men in the front of the room, as well as about 25 to 30 other people, presumably from various law enforcement agencies.

FBI agent Darren Miller stopped what he was doing, looked around the room a couple times, looked at me and said, "if everyone will take their seat and get comfortable, we will begin. Chief of Police Hanson sends his regrets but he is still in Hartford on police business and the weather will delay his returning. In the room we have Mr. Johnny Hamilton, Mr. & Mrs. Montgomery Walker, Mrs. Stephanie Hunter, Esq., Mr. & Mrs. Carl Walker, and Dr. Gerald Walker. We also have members of various state and federal agencies represented, and I will not take the time to go through all those names and agencies with you now. Standing next to me is Mr. Devon Miller from the National Security Administration, or NSA. If he looks familiar, it is because you are looking at me...not really. Devon is my younger brother and, by some weird stroke of luck, was assigned to work on an investigation that eventually crossed paths with our investigation." Agent Darren Miller looked around the room for a moment and said, "oh, Momma would be so proud!" That comment brought several chuckles from the group.

NSA agent Miller then talked about why his agency is investigating what appears to be a local PD, or at most a state crime; that is the murder of the Keeper family. Apparently Gilbert Keeper, one of the four Keeper children, has been selling corporate secrets to the Chinese government, as well as obtaining very confidential data and secret data from sources in the U.S. government, and selling that data, also. He has many contacts in China, Russia and several other countries, and used many of these contacts for his sales of data. On top of this, came the theft of million of dollars from his employer, and a couple of the companies that they dealt with. Gilbert Keeper was tried on these and several unrelated counts, such as attempted murder, false imprisonment, bodily injury, destruction of private property, and a whole long list of charges. As Mrs. Hunter can attest, he was a pretty bad hombre."

With that statement, Mrs. Walker, who is sitting next to Stephanie, reached over to hold Stephanie's hand in comfort. Several people in front of Stephanie turned to look back at her and smile.

Agent Miller continued, "Gilbert Keeper was tried, convicted and sentenced to spend the rest of his life behind bars, plus an additional 40 or 50 years, and that's just on the Federal charges. The state of Connecticut has not filed all their charges against him, yet. Gilbert Keeper was being transported to the Allenwood, PA high security men's prison in central Pennsylvania when an auto accident with the prison van caused two prison guards, and one convict to die. Gilbert Keeper, and one other convict, a Manuel Valasquez, managed to escape."

With that bit of news, Mrs. Walker's grip on Stephanie's hand became much tighter as she looked at Stephanie's face. Stephanie's eyes had started to form tears, but she did not say or do anything.

I immediately asked the agent if both men have been recaptured. Agent Miller looked around the room as if he was trying to get some nod from someone before saying "no. Both men are still on the run and both are considered dangerous. Manuel Valasquez is a convicted murderer, rapist, and was found guilty of torturing his victims quite cruelly."

"Are they traveling together?" I asked. "Does your department know their whereabouts?"

"Our latest information," agent Miller answered, "shows that Gilbert Keeper has crossed over into Canada, and may have gotten passage aboard an oil tanker bound for Kuwait. We are attempting to track down our leads right now. Manuel Valasquez was last sighted in Topeka, Kansas and is believed to be headed either for the west coast, or for Mexico where he has many relatives. Our bet is Mexico."

I raised my hand to ask a question that I wasn't certain I wanted to know the answer to. "When did these two men escape, agent Miller? Seems like you might need a fair amount of time to go from mid-Pennsylvania, to Topeka, Kansas."

Both the FBI and the NSA agents Miller looked at each other and sort of did a little shuffle with their shoes

"Well," FBI agent Miller said, "it has been nine and one half days since the collision with the van occurred. They have had plenty of time to make their getaways."

"Nine and one half days," Stephanie said, "and, we are just hearing about this now?"

FBI agent Miller said that department policy is to try to confirm leads and start country-wide alerts, and searches of probable destinations before alerting other people to an event. They, apparently, have been trying to recapture both fugitives before word got out.

"From the little I know of what Derek and Stephanie Hunter went through at the hands of Gilbert Keeper," I said, "I think your agency policy is certainly doing a disservice to them, and perhaps many other potential victims."

"We want everyone to be aware, and involved while the search for both men goes forward." Says FBI agent Miller. "We also want everyone to be safe and aware that Gilbert Keeper, in particular, knows this area, has ties to this area, and may try to come back to this area. He has been motivated by something that he believes is within the Victorian mansion owned by the Hunters. Now, in addition to Mr. & Mrs. Hunter, we now have Mr. & Mrs. Walker living in the house. Mr. Hamilton, we have discovered that your very ill wife' s maiden name was Keeper. Do not know if you are aware of that, or not, but that will put you in harms' way, and Mrs. Carla Walker, being Mr. Hamilton's sister puts you and your husband in jeopardy. Other members of the family may be brought into the 'circle of harm' simply by being related. This guy is on the run and we don't know what he is capable of, so we want everyone here, and other family members to act like they are being put in danger; because they could be."

After everyone had shifted their bodies in their chairs, we all started looking at each other with that expression of uncertainty on our faces. What will this mean for us? How will this change our lives? Who will win the Super Bowl this time? Where's Waldo?

Stephanie asked agent Miller what type of precautions all of the family members should be taking. Agent Miller went through the standard array of answers about being aware of your surroundings, traveling in two's, or more, not allowing yourself to be in a location that you cannot escape from, and a list of others.

Then Stephanie asked if the FBI was in contact with the oil tanker that Gilbert Keeper is believed to be aboard, to which agent Miller said that they have been in touch with the captain of the ship but that he has denied any Americans being onboard. It seems that the ship is in international waters, and is sailing under a Chinese flag which means little, or no cooperation from the crew. Apparently the FBI is asking for help from the international community, but it is possible that Gilbert Keeper has more friends abroad than the bureau has. The FBI has people heading for Kuwait to await the arrival of the oil tanker, but for right now they have no confirmation that Keeper is actually onboard.

FBI agent Miller could sense the tension rising within our family members as he tried to calm things down. He advised us all that the agency will have agents shadowing us day and night and will be completely invisible to us in our daily lives. This is in addition to the international, and domestic, searching going on for both escapees. He reminded Stephanie how quickly the FBI swooped in at her house when Keeper had her and her husband captive.

I could tell by looking at Stephanie's face that agent Miller's talk was not all the reassurance that she needed to feel completely safe.

The meeting continued for another twenty minutes before ending and everyone went back to their daily lives. Stephanie said that she was going to host dinner for everyone at her house at six this evening. She hoped that everyone would be able to make it, but warned that it was being catered, and with that, everyone would be safe from her, or Derek's, cooking. Everyone said that they would be there and, of course, asked what they could bring to help with the meal. "Not a thing," Stephanie replied, "we are having the new French restaurant handle everything. We also will have 'French Mac-n-Cheese' for the children, too, along with non-alcoholic champagne for them." This was a special treat for Dr. Gerald Walker's four children who Derek said always seem to get stuck with "always having to settle for adult food."

As I headed for the entrance I told Stephanie that I would be there, but I have a meeting with the doctors regarding Sally's status and future care. She put her arm around my shoulders and asked if I wanted her to go with me for support. "Thank you for offering, but no. Carla and Carl are going to be there with me, and I don't want to outnumber the doctors."

"What about any legal decision that you may have to make," Stephanie asked, "do you want me to keep my phone close by?"

I thanked her and said that might be a good idea, just in case. We reached the front entrance to the police headquarters to see a torrential downpour of rain coming down outside. Just then a double explosion of lightning and extremely loud thunder startled everyone, and I began to wonder if I should go, or stay. "Should I go or should I stay?" I have heard those words before.

I glanced at my watch and saw that the time had come for me to head to the hospital. I knew driving time would be doubled, or more, due to the bad weather, so I grabbed my phone and placed a call to Dr. Chambers. I gave him my status and said I was on my way. He said he would alert the other doctors so that everyone would be available, including Dr. Eldon, the Chief of Staff.

By the time I got to my car I was completely drenched clear down to my skin. An umbrella and a raincoat did not seem to be much protection against the torrential downpour. The lightning was striking close by which made the thunder almost instantaneous and extremely loud when it cracked.

I was certainly glad to be inside my car and not still trying to get into it. I watched the rain for a minute, as if I expected it to suddenly stop so that I could continue on, and saw the agents Miller and Miller leave the safety and dryness of the police building and get into a black, unmarked SUV. Guess I watch too much TV because I would have guessed correctly that that was a Federal vehicle even before I saw them get into it. Dead giveaway those black SUV's with small red and blue lights slightly visible. Dead giveaway.

I put my car into 'drive' and left the parking lot heading across town to the hospital. Travel was perilous and slow, even on a Thursday afternoon, due to the downpour. I arrived at the hospital still drenched from my earlier shower, and decided I could not get much wetter. Opening the door of my car I bolted for the main entrance to the hospital. That short run confirmed that when a body is drenched to the skin, it cannot get any wetter. As I walked inside, the hospital crew had laid a long stretch of carpeting down so that anyone who would dare be outside on a day like today, would not be subjected to wet, slippery floors upon entering. The hospital set up a temporary 'cloak room' so that people entering could leave wet coats and umbrellas there.

I found Dr. Chambers rather easily, and we headed to a conference room where the other doctors awaited. We walked in to a group of three specialists and Dr. Helen Eldon, the hospital's Chief of Staff. I had met everyone previously, so introductions were skipped and conversation went directly to my wife's condition. Dr. Chambers started things off with a recap of Sally's arrival date and condition at that time, and brought both areas up to today. With input from the other doctors, including a neurologist, the discussion continued on for over an hour. When everyone had expressed their learned opinions, the 'question on the table' was whether, or not, to take my wife off the life support machines that, without a doubt, were keeping her alive. Even though the Walkers have picked up the medical expenses above what the insurance companies cover, the expenses will continue to climb, and climb. How much added expense can they pick up before it burdens even them?

I knew that a decision had to be made, but I was having more difficulty making it than I ever thought I would.

I had heard from everyone, had to factor everyone's input, but had not heard a word from Dr. Eldon.

"Doctor Eldon," I started, "you have not expressed any thoughts regarding this matter, and I value your opinion. How are you leaning as it pertains to my wife, Sally?"

Doctor Eldon sat motionless for a while looking directly into my eyes before speaking. "I do not have to make this decision. This is not my loved one who is being kept alive by unnatural means, but, I would allow her the opportunity of life. Whether by machines, or by natural means, I would allow her to be kept alive." Just then Dr. Eldon received an urgent page and had to excuse herself as she got up from the table and left the room.

I was no closer to a decision after Dr. Eldon's input, but knew the 'clock was ticking'. I looked at the faces of the doctors sitting at the table; I looked out the window at the downpour of rain that only got heavier and did not seem to be lessening any. I looked at everything around me except the choices I have. Finally I asked Dr. Chambers when they had to know my decision.

"It's something that you need to do sooner, rather than later because if your wife is going to be able to support her life systems without the aid of mechanical equipment, than she will take some time to prove it. If we 'pull the plugs' today, it may be 48 hours, it may be a week before we know how she will do. That's a big unknown." Dr. Chamber answered.

"I have a family dinner to go to now, I will sleep on this and give you my decision in the morning." I told the doctors. "Should I call you, Doctor Chambers?"

He said 'yes', and thanked me and the other doctors for attending and for giving their expert input. I thanked everyone and headed for the cloak room to retrieve my umbrella and rain coat before exiting outside to the torrential rain and wind.

As I walked along in the hallway I noticed a door lettered "Chief of Staff.' I tried to open it but found it locked and secure. I wanted to simply thank Dr. Eldon before I left, so I went into the adjoining door marked "Office." Inside sat a nice, elderly volunteer woman who said that Dr. Eldon would be returning any moment and I could wait for her if I wanted. Since I had a few spare minutes before I should be leaving for Stephanie & Derek's house, I told the lady I would wait for the doctor.

I took a seat and started checking emails on my cell phone because I knew that with this terrible storm, something was bound to happen. The volunteer excused herself for a minute and left the office to go down the hallway for a couple minutes. It was after she left that I thought I heard voices coming from the inner office and figured Dr. Eldon had entered through the other doorway. I rose from my chair and stuck my head through the partially opened door leading to Dr. Eldon's office. To my surprise, the office appeared to be empty. I stepped into the office and heard the voices even more plainly. There on a shelf in one of two built-in bookshelves, was a radio tuned to a station conducting some political interviews. With the radio volume low, it sounded like people talking from within the office. As I turned to leave the office I couldn't help but notice all the awards, and plaques of achievements lining the doctor's office walls; quite a record of achievement and service to the medical field and her community. Among all the awards, were the doctor's various college diplomas showing her outstanding progress in various medical specialties.

Just as I was admiring the assortment of pictures and plaques on her office walls, the lady volunteer came through the doorway saying "Sir, this is a private office and you are not supposed to be in here without the doctor!"

"I understand, and I'm sorry. I thought I heard Dr. Eldon talking in here, and since the door was opened, I stuck my head in to see her. It was her radio that I heard, not people talking in here. Again, I'm sorry. I'm also running out of time and have to be down in Westport shortly. Would you please tell Dr. Eldon that Johnny Hamilton stopped by to see her and I will talk to her another time?" I said.

Lady volunteer said she would give Dr. Eldon my message and that she did not envy me having to drive in the terrible storm we were having.

I agreed with her and turned to exit the office.

And, there it is! Like a flashing neon sign! On the wall for all the world to see! Proud as can be! A diploma from the College of Medicine, Stanford

University, Stanford, California. Nicely signed by four people of high esteem within the university and medical fields. Issued to one 'Helen Louisa Eldon.' Helen Louisa.

I barely noticed that I had stopped breathing until my forehead starting pounding against my ear drums. I caught my breath and said "Good night" to the lady volunteer.

The wind had become much stronger, and the rain was much more intense since I had arrived at the hospital, which made driving a very slow, difficult endeavor. I wondered as I drove why Dr. Eldon had been so quiet and detached from the discussions and why she, seemingly, avoided giving me her opinion. Maybe now I know. Maybe she and my wife were, or are, related.

Arriving at Stephanie & Derek's Victorian, I was glad to see the wind and the rain had lessened substantially. Only a short distance from Bridgeport to Westport, but almost a world away, weather wise.

Stephanie met me at the front door, took my coat and umbrella, and escorted me to the living room. Almost everyone else was here already except Dr. Gerald and his family. They had the greatest distance to travel, and the most little people to get ready to travel, so additional time for he and his family was a given.

Carla and Carl immediately asked me how the meeting at the hospital had gone and if there was any improvement in Sally's condition. I filled them in on the meeting, the discussions, the decision I must make by tomorrow, and that there is no change in Sally. They both wished me luck and said that they are available if I need them for anything; anything, at all. I also told them I have major news for our investigation and have solved one of the missing links we had. This really piqued their curiosity and they wanted to be filled in right away, but I told them we would talk later and not ruin Derek and Stephanie's dinner now.

I was surprised to see Andrew Walker and his wife Agnes there because they rarely are in town whenever a family get-together happens. Andrew owns one of the world's largest precious metals firms in the world, and is constantly traveling for his business. His wife Agnes is able to travel with him and handles some small   jobs for the company.

Also present is Andrea (Walker) Stevens, a Walker daughter, and one of the top physicist in the world. Her husband, Andrew, a research biologist, is on an assignment for the government of Brazil and will not return home for another seven weeks. This dinner is beginning to be bigger than the size of the group for Mr. Walker's birthday party.

After Dr. Gerald and his family arrived, and everyone had some libations within them, Stephanie announced that dinner was being served. Libations in hand, everyone headed for the dining room and a grand, catered, dinner. The children really like Stephanie's arrangement for dinner because they get to sit at the same table as the adults.

Dinner was excellent and everyone was very happy and content to sit back and relax afterwards. Derek had set up children's movies in Stephanie's office, and video games in his office for the children's entertainment. It did not take them long to decide their choices and start playing while the adults took their after-dinner drinks and retired to the family room.

With everyone relaxed and enjoying conversation, Stephanie took advantage of the opportunity to tell the rest of the family about the meeting earlier today with the FBI and Police department. She told them about Gilbert Keeper's escape and how every member of the family could be in peril. She gave everyone, who was not present at the meeting, one of FBI Agent Miller's business cards with the phone number highlighted. We all discussed Gilbert Keeper and what little we know about his location, and how we must be in touch with each other much more often. Keep track of children, spouses, pets, everything.

As the time got later and later, people started gathering things and getting ready to leave. Children were getting tired, some older adults were getting tired, and with Stephanie and Derek having the meal catered, there was not dish one to worry about for anyone.

After everyone else had left, and Mr. & Mrs. Walker had retired to the third floor, Carla asked me what did I learn at the hospital. Unsure of where to begin, I took a deep breath and told Carla, Carl, and Stephanie about Sally and the decision to be made. I talked about her physical condition and the fact that she was only alive by artificial means. Stephanie asked me if I had made any decision yet, or if I was going to sleep on it and decide in the morning. I have decided to sleep on it. The real news was in taking everyone back to our investigations in the attic and the documents that referenced a 'Helen Louisa' something, and then later, a 'Helen Louisa Jessup.' I told them about seeing all the awards and diplomas on the walls in Dr. Eldon's office at the hospital, including her medical degree from Stanford University issued to one 'Helen Louisa Eldon.'

I again took a deep breath, looking at each face, and said "now, what if? Remember the handwritten notes we found which made no sense at all? What if...one note applied to Gilbert Keeper, and another note applied to Dr. Helen Eldon. For example: Gilbert Keeper, a rising star in politics, almost guaranteed the Governor's office and simply drops out of politics completely and goes into accounting. Note that applies? 'politico - NO!'" With that statement everyone started looking at each other with inquisitive looks on their faces.

I followed up with "now, suppose again that another note might apply to Dr. Eldon. The note that applies? ' medical gotcha.' It seems as logical as anything that I can think of, especially after seeing Dr. Eldon's full name on her wall: Helen Louisa Eldon."

Carl did not agree with my thinking. He thought that both were too much of a stretch to be real. Stephanie, on the other hand, said she thought each note could easily apply to each person, but wondered why a 'Jessup' was among all the 'Keeper' children. With raised eyebrows, and a slight smile, Stephanie said that her law firm had a team of interns doing ancestral research for a client involved in a mega-million dollar lawsuit. She was texting someone on her phone, when she told us that they would do some ancestral searching for the Keepers, and the Jessups to see if there were any connections.

Derek came out of his office long enough to say good night to everyone and headed off to the second floor. He had to catch an early flight in the morning to Chicago so had to call it an early evening.

Stephanie offered everyone a final cup of coffee or tea before heading out into the stormy night. We all decided that another cup, after several glasses of wine earlier with dinner, would be a good idea.

By the time Stephanie had served everyone their tea and coffee, she was getting replies back on her phone from her earlier text message. She joked as she typed to an intern that they were not supposed to be in the office this late at night, but was informed that this young lady was working on the research at home in her apartment. Stephanie thanked her and told her that any time tomorrow would be fine; just fit it into her other tasks as time allows.

The intern texted Stephanie that she already had found information about the ancestry of both the Keepers and the Jessups, and would email her a synopsis of her findings in a few minutes. She would also continue researching both families tomorrow as time allowed her to. Stephanie thanked her and said goodnight.

Stephanie told us all of her intern's findings and said she would forward the email on to us after she receives it.

With that, we all said 'thank you' to Stephanie for hosting dinner, and everything else, and donned our raincoats and umbrellas.

CHAPTER 14

I phoned Dr. Chambers three days ago and told him I wanted to give Sally's body the chance to do its' job the way it is supposed to do it. I feel it is inhuman to keep her connected to machines that do all the work for her, so I want her off the life support system. Dr. Chambers said he would do as I wish, and will send me an email with all her vitals at the moment she is disconnected. I then sat in my car in my garage for a long time wondering if I had really done the right thing, or not.

I talked to Dr. Chambers before I left on another 'road trip.' I had to check in on our new branches, and our newest manager in our Springfield branch, Sumner Adams. Sumner had the interview that I set up for him, and impressed the directors with his knowledge and experience. The problem for Sumner was that one of the Royal Bank management people saw him in NYC and saw him go into the CitiCorp building. One question led to another question which led to Sumner being fired. To Sumner's credit, he never lied to anyone, he never denied that he had been approached by Citibank. Already, he says, his life has gotten better, and he is beginning to talk with his wife about moving back to Springfield. He has told me that his wife has not said "yes" to this idea yet, but is no longer saying "absolutely not!"

The Springfield branch was doing very well; it was now the 'premier financial' establishment in the city according to the Boston newspapers and their financial writers. Sumner's staff was very well trained and knowledgeable and customers simply liked doing business with us. This was a good move on our 'collective' part.

I had taken I-90 west from Springfield over to Albany, New York and dropped in on our branch there. This is another branch now managed by a former Royal Bank manager, and is doing very well. I planned on spending the night in Albany before continuing on to Utica, New York in the morning. I wanted to look at a couple locations where we could possibly open a small, sort of satellite type, branch to serve what was becoming a growing area.

I had just checked into my motel room when my cell phone rang. Looking at the caller ID, and seeing that it was a "blocked caller", I decided to let the call go to voice mail while I prepared a quick and easy dinner for myself. Gone were those days past of 'TV Dinners', todays 'microwaveable' meals were, for the most part, decent tasting and quick-to-prepare.

While I enjoyed my salad and pasta meal, I decided to check the voice mail message from the previous 'blocked' caller. It was Dr. Chambers informing me that Sally had finally given in to her injuries and peacefully passed away late this afternoon. The doctor gave me all her vitals that were taken about 90 minutes before her heart gave out so I would have the information for my file I was keeping. I listened to the doctor's message three times before I realized that I was sitting at the little desk/table in the room, with a mouthful of food, not knowing whether to chew it, swallow it, or what to do. I was in a mild trance and undecided what to do next.

It seemed in my mind, that life was still moving forward as long as Sally was still alive. As long as she still had a beating heart, blood pumping through her body, breath going into her lungs, life was still bearable; but, now what? What do I do now when the last member, my loving spouse, the mother of my children, my life partner had died? Suddenly, I was alone; all alone. I had lost three children and my wife.

Dr. Chambers had also said that Dr. Helen Eldon has been missing for almost four days. Her husband, and the administrators of the medical centers have not been able to locate her, or reach her by cell phone. She was making her rounds with a group of visiting doctors from the United Nations, went to lunch with them in the hospital's VIP dining hall, and an hour later could not be found. Dr. Chambers wondered if I had any thoughts as to where she may have gone.

I forgot about Dr. Chambers, Dr. Eldon, and all else. I simply sat and stared at the blank motel room wall as I remembered Sally's soft skin, beautiful green eyes, and the smell of her hair. Her gentle touch was felt on my left cheek, and it startled me and snapped me back into reality. Dr. Chambers was continuing on with other questions, but he seemed to be speaking in a foreign language; I could not understand what he was saying. Suddenly he had a mouth full of food and was trying to talk and chew and everything else, all at the same time. The room started spinning as I tried to grasp some words Dr. Chambers was telling me, and then, suddenly, the room spun out of control and the lights went out.

I do not know what time it is right now. I do not know what strange room I am in, and I continue to stare at the ceiling. I do not know who this strange man is that is looking down at me asking me something with a language I do not understand. Another strange man stares down at me from the other side, and now a female is looking down at me. She seems to be twenty feet tall. Someone is pushing me and trying to force me upright. All I can do is wonder why all these people are here; and where is here?

"Damn, that hurts!" I yell at one man, "what are you trying to do?" Now I realize he just gave me some kind of shot in my arm. The woman is feeling my left breast; no, she is checking my heart rate and has a stethoscope there. Slowly, oh so slowly the vision is returning and I can tell that the man giving me the shot, and the twenty foot tall woman are EMT responders who are attending to me.

"What's going on?" I ask. "What happened and where am I?" These are the questions that come out of my mouth while I begin to see the whole picture more clearly. They manage to get me into a sitting position on the floor as the woman tells someone what my vitals are. I look around and ask the man with another needle in his hand what has happened and why are all these people here. AND, where is here?

Little by little things start to come into focus and I see another man that I have seen before, He is telling me that he is the manager and he was walking past my room when he heard a loud thud sound like something, or someone, had fallen. He knocked several times but got no response. He said he was concerned because he heard the TV set and could not get any one to answer. He cautiously opened the door and found me passed out on the floor with spilled food all over me and a cell phone laying next to my body. He then called 9-1-1.

By the time he had finished his short story, I was focusing sharply on things, and people, in the room and was feeling like I was human again. The EMT fellow was telling me that something caused me to have acute anxiety to the point of passing out. He asked me if I remembered what caused the anxiety attack. I told him I did; I had gotten a voicemail message from my wife's doctor in Bridgeport that she had died. While I listened to his message, I kept having flashbacks of times with my wife and children, who had also died recently. I kept having difficulty breathing and getting dizzy, and guessed that I had passed out.

The motel manager said that when he picked up my cell phone off the floor that there was some doctor on the line saying my name over and over. The manager told the doctor what was going on and the doctor said that he was in Bridgeport and could not assist. That was when the manager phoned 911.

I thanked everyone for coming to my aid but I felt like my old self again and would probably just get some water and rest. The EMT fellow said that state law required them to take me to the closest emergency room for evaluation and release by a licensed doctor, so no water yet, and no going to bed. Yet.

As I stood up I saw it was twenty minutes past two in the morning, which meant I had been unconscious for somewhere between four and six hours. Now everything was together again and I was remembering the message left by Dr. Chambers regarding Sally and the small things I remembered that started my difficulty with my breathing, and the room spinning. Now everything was clear again. Now I was being positioned on an ambulance gurney for a ride to the emergency ward at a local hospital.

I was guessing that my stops in Utica later this morning would have to be postponed; perhaps until my next trip up here.

I also guessed that I might miss the motel's 'check out time' and asked the manager if he would lock the room and keep it for me until I returned later. He assured me that he would.

# CHAPTER 15

Have I said previously how much I hate ANY medical environment? Well let me say it again! Even when I am the one who is being treated, and I know it is for my benefit that I endure the environment, I simply do not like the smell, the décor, the aromas of blood, harsh cleansers, sweat, floor wax and anesthetics. Yes, the people are nice. The people want to help heal me. The people are well trained and caring, but, NO, I don't like medical environments.

After all treatments were completed, and all forms were signed so that they could bill my insurance company, the ER physician discharged me. His parting words were about getting more rest and relaxation than I have been getting, and to see my regular family physician when I get home. Family physician? Family? Well, I won't bother him with my tale of woe.

I made it back to the motel and retrieved my belongings. I stopped by the office to tell the night manager "thank you" for all that he did last night to help me. Had he not been close by and heard what he thought was a strange noise coming from my room, who knows where I would be today.

To my surprise, he was still working; doing a double shift to help another manager and to get some much needed extra money. I thanked him profusely and told him I would be checking out shortly, but would be back again in about a week and a half. He thought I ought to use my room to get some extra sleep before driving back to Bridgeport, but I told him I had personal business there that would not wait.

After I downed two cups of coffee from the breakfast buffet area, I packed my travel bag and gathered my papers. The drive home would be both good news and bad; good that I am able to travel once again, and bad because of what awaits me when I get to Bridgeport. I now need to make funeral arrangements for Sally. Am I making funeral arrangements for Sally Hamilton or for Sally Keeper? The questions running through my head are tremendous and forced me to slow down to a speed that allows me to think and be aware of my driving.

Again, as they had before, those thoughts of Sally rushed through my head. I remembered the softness of her skin, and the smell of her hair. I remembered how her beautiful green eyes would sparkle when she giggled, and how ticklish she was when we used to laugh and wrestle like children. Whoever she was, Hamilton or Keeper or whomever, she was an amazing mother who took care of her children's every need. She was an intelligent, warm, caring and giving woman who enriched the lives of many, many people.

She was also someone else! Someone whose entire childhood had been built upon lies; lies to me, lies to friends, and lies to everyone that had ever come into contact with her. Beyond her childhood, her entire life was built upon a composition of lies and falsehoods. I am wondering who she ever told the truth to.

It seemed like a long drive back to Bridgeport, but I know it seemed that way only because I was physically tired and emotionally drained. Otherwise, it would have gone by much faster. The normal four hour drive took me nearly five and one-half hours to negotiate the I-90 eastbound, and then south on state route 8 to home.

As I pulled onto my street I could see both Carl and Carla's car, and the car of Mr. & Mrs. Walker parked in front of my house. As I started to wonder why they would be there waiting on me, I guessed that either the doctor from the emergency ward in Utica, or Dr. Chambers had called Carla and given her the news regarding Sally. My bet was on Dr. Chambers.

I pulled my car into the garage and allowed the garage door to close completely before getting out of the car with my travel bag and attaché. I went into the kitchen through the inside garage door and was immediately grabbed by Carla and given a huge, nearly bone-crushing hug. She was sobbing profusely and whispering in my ear how sorry she was about Sally. It wasn't more than fifteen to twenty seconds before Carl and Mrs. Walker were also giving me hugs and tears of consolation.

After several minutes everyone pulled away and reached for tissues to wipe tears away and take care of runny noses. When everyone had cleared away, Mr. Walker came over to me and quietly said to me "Johnny, you are strong beyond belief, and you know when to release everything pent up inside. I wish I could take away all your pain, but I can't. I am here right beside you, though, when you need help." And, with that Mr. Walker gave me a hug that did have all of my vertebrae in my spine cracking and popping. I suddenly felt like I had come home to my family and let more tears flow, unabashed.

After a couple minutes, Mr. Walker stepped back and looked deeply and long into my eyes. He then gave me a handshake that had my hand feeling as though it was caught in a bench vise. I grabbed a stool at the kitchen counter and sat down before my knees started to buckle and my legs give out.

Carla asked me if I wanted a glass of wine, or a cup of freshly-made coffee. I answered that the wine sounds very tempting, but I would probably be asleep within five minutes. She poured me a full mug of coffee and settled in to talk about things.

Apparently the ER doctor in Utica called Dr. Chambers and told him about my 'episode' there, and Dr. Chambers called Carla to advise her as to what happened. Carla then let the rest of the family know.

I tried, without a lot of success, to express my gratitude to everyone for them being there when I got home from Utica. I talked about how the wave of emotions came over me when I received the news about Sally, and how I could not hold back the feelings about her, even knowing the dark truth about her past years. I talked and talked about how the feelings of days gone by caught up with me as I remembered good times, times of intimacy, and times that the two of us spent with our kids. The same kids who were also dead.

Once a family of five, and now a family of one. And the song that has the words in it of "one is the loneliest number that you'll ever meet" is absolutely right! A family of one can hardly be called a family. More like a single man, a widower, a bachelor, or ONE. The idea of my family shrinking in size so rapidly, so horribly bothered me so deeply that it was as if some grotesque being was eating through my soul and chewing upon my bone marrow.

"Right now," I told everyone, "I just need to make arrangements for Sally, get my head together, and keep working. I will make it through this." I managed a small smile for everyone's benefit and took a long sip of my coffee.

As we drank our cups of coffee we discussed funeral arrangements for Sally. Carl and Carla said that, if I would allow them, they would take care of everything with the funeral home and cemetery.

They would check with me before ordering casket, headstone or anything, but would handle making all arrangements and scheduling the service. I thanked them and told them how much I would appreciate them doing that.

The following two weeks went by in the blink of an eye and the service for Sally was nice. The weather did not cooperate though as the remains of a severe hurricane that swept up the east coast came into Long Island sound and pounded the Connecticut coast. It was the weather that kept most of our friends away from the funeral home and, at the last moment, caused the graveside service to be postponed. Our retired family priest said that he had never seen a storm this severe in all his 84 years.

The following week the weather had calmed down and things were back to normal. Carl had asked me about helping set up a new branch outside my territory in Harrisburg, PA. I told him I would be glad to assist and would refill my travel bag and meet him there.

Going north around New York and picking up I-78 in eastern Pennsylvania shortened the drive time except for having to stop and pay tolls.

Even at that it was a nice drive and I was able to stop and eat a late lunch at an old-fashioned roadside 'diner' that I thought had disappeared many years ago. I believe people call this type of food "comfort food." It was good, and there was way too much of it for my stomach.

I arrived in Harrisburg early evening and checked into my room that Carl had reserved for me at the Hilton Hotel near the Whitaker Center. A four star hotel with large rooms, and an acclaimed chef and restaurant. Carl had already left a voicemail for me saying that he was buying drinks, and maybe even dinner, in the bar off the lobby when I got my stuff settled. I know when to accept an invitation, or not, so I hung my suit and shirts up in the closet and headed back downstairs to find Carl.

Finding Carl in a lounge full of businessmen was not difficult; he was sitting at the bar talking financial matters with another man when I walked up. He introduced me to the other man who had the face of someone that I knew from years gone by. His name, Tim Kendall, did not ring any bells, but his face certainly did as the three of us sat and talked about a myriad of topics. Finally Tim said he had to go meet his fiancé and her parents for dinner and we all exchanged business cards with a promise that he would look for our new branch bank when he returned to Harrisburg.

The following morning we met with a realtor who had several locations for sale that he was eager to discuss. As we went from location to location, the face of Tim Kendall kept coming back into focus. Finally the last location that the realtor showed to Carl and I was nearly perfect. It had been a bank many years ago, and, to the owner's credit, had been well maintained since then. The latest occupant had been a pizza parlor, which had done so well that they outgrew the facility and had to relocate to a much larger building.

We decided to have a beer at a local pub and discuss the fine details with the realtor. The discussion went back and forth until he quoted a price that Carl was happy with. Carl had him sign an agreement to sell and gave him a copy, and asked that he be available tomorrow when the corporate realty offices phoned to confirm the purchase.

Carl and I went back to our hotel so he could email the agreement to sell to the Board and to the realty department at corporate. Having fully utilized the business center at the Hilton Hotel, Carl said that he would buy dinner if I had the time. I gladly accepted and asked Carl if HE had the time of if he should be heading home to Carla. He said that Carla was on the west coast again, trying to straighten out some problems at one of their subsidiaries; so he was a bachelor this week and would be staying over tonight before heading back to New York.

I drove back to Bridgeport making several stops along the way at our various branches. The only problem within these branches was with my manager of our Danbury branch. I felt something was very wrong with him, either physically or in his personal life, and wanted to get to the bottom of things before I had to fire him. I timed my arrival for a few minutes after eleven so I could spend a few minutes talking bank business and then take him out for lunch to get more into other matters.

I asked Fred, the branch manager, to have lunch with me, and got a "sorry, I can't" reply from him. I thought for a minute before asking him why, only to get a "personal business that I have to take care of" answer. I had never played my "I'm the boss" card, but now I would.

I took Fred off to the side of a vacant area of the branch and told him "it's either lunch with me, now, or breakfast at the unemployment department tomorrow." Suddenly Fred had the time for lunch and we left to go around the corner to a quiet eatery where I could get a isolated booth for the two of us. After we ordered our meals, I told Fred how his banking business was off, how poor his weekly reports were, and how the corporate office wanted me to replace him right away. Customers had been making negative comments about his branch on the company website, and it was my job to find out what was wrong and fix it.

Fred sat and listened without comments for a while and finally, after his eyes started welling up with tears, told me that he was having marital problems. Apparently Fred's wife, Alice, who is from southern California, was not adapting well to the Danbury, Connecticut environment and really hated the long, cold winters here. She was talking about taking their four children back to the sun and warmth of her beach community in California. This had been creating a lot of strife between husband and wife, and Fred had let it get into his work environment, also. Alice was calling him at the branch all day long and starting arguments with him, and this, Fred believes, is why his mind has not been on his job recently. He was hoping to get things worked out before his poor performance was noticed by corporate.

I made a quick phone call to corporate Human Resources department and got the number of vacation days that Fred was entitled to. After that Fred and I talked a long while about how difficult it can be for a family to acclimate to an east coast area when they have not lived in one before. Winters can be tough and cruel in some cities, and in others winters can be even worst.

After two hours of lunch and talking, I asked how Fred's assistant manager was doing and could he manage the branch for a couple days. Fred extolled the virtues and expertise of his assistant manager, and gave him much of the credit for the branch doing well in spite of Fred's preoccupation with personal problems.

I told Fred that when we got back to the branch I wanted him to turn over the branch to his assistant, and take a two week vacation with his wife and children, if possible, and work things out with his wife. Whatever it takes to get his personal life put back in order had greater priority now than did the branch, and even if his wife ends up returning to California, Fred needs to get himself in a better mental frame of mind. I told him some about Sumner Adams and the problems he went through with his Georgia-born wife, and how that situation played out.

On the walk back to the branch, Fred thanked me for talking with him and for giving him the opportunity to get his personal matters straightened out. When we arrived at the branch Fred called his assistant into his office and the three of us had a brief meeting before I left for home. I really hope that Fred can get everything put in order and I don't have to replace an educated, personable, experienced manager.

# CHAPTER 16

I had decided several weeks ago to put my large, somewhat empty house on the market. Selling it would allow me to downsize, or, more appropriately, move into a townhouse sized just right for me. Being a family of one was not what I intended, but living alone in a much-too-large a home was not among my intentions, either.

I hired a professional cleaning firm to come in and clean, paint, and 'stage' the home like a show home would be. They also moved all my furniture into two storage units at the local 'Extra Space Storage' location. All this was occurring while I was making my road trips so that when I returned, I walked into a completely new, someone-else's, house. Sparkling clean, new modern furniture, and a choice location within a great school district; I had no doubts that it would not take long to sell my house.

In the meantime, Stephanie and Derek were kind enough to offer me a guest room at their house while I investigated some new townhomes being built on the coastline overlooking Black Rock Harbor. I gladly accepted their offer and gathered up my personal items for moving. Although it would be a little bit strange living in their home with a married couple, and their married in-laws one floor above me, I expected to be gone much of the time travelling around to the branches. And, it will only be for a very short time, anyway.

The first week living at the Victorian known as 'Keeper House' went great; I was in the guest room a total of two hours. The remainder of the week I was in New York City for a management meeting, and visiting various branches. The second week I was there only about a half-day longer having to go back to Danbury and manage the branch while we got the new manager, the former assistant manager, up to speed with items he had not been exposed to before Fred's departure.

Yes, Fred decided that his family was more important than his career with Citibank, and moved everyone back to southern California. My loss, his loss. One thing he was correct about was the ability of his assistant and it didn't take me long to have him up to speed with our procedures and tasks.

Driving back to Bridgeport I received a phone call from both my realtor telling me that we had a solid offer on my house, and from the agent for the developer of the Black Rock Harbor Townhouses saying that the model townhouse I really liked had become available, again. Two good phone calls make for a great ending to any day.

As I pulled my car into the driveway at the Victorian, I did not see any other cars parked there. I grabbed my travel bag and attaché from the trunk and headed for the house. As I got closer to the back door I started to notice a faint smell of old, rotten meat. This was not something I had ever smelled before, but it got stronger and stronger as I reached the back door.

The house was completely dark, which surprised me since Stephanie had put timers and light-sensitive controllers and lamps on every floor since their big problem with the Guido fellow. As I put my key into the lock of the back door, I noticed how strong the rotten meat smell had become, and I saw what appeared to be the beam of a flashlight bouncing off walls in different rooms. Oh, great! I thought, the power has gone out and I have computer work I have to get done tonight.

My key was not needed as the door was not closed completely. I pushed the door open knowing that Stephanie or Derek was inside trying to figure out what caused their power outage. I walked in and called out for Derek or Stephanie as I went into the back porch area feeling my way toward the flashlight, which was always plugged into an electrical outlet there.

The rotten meat smell was now overpowering and rather nauseating as I found the outlet empty of any flashlight. Okay, I thought, I'll get the one out of my travel bag and use it. Setting my bags down I retrieved my 'travel-along' flashlight from one bag and started to look around the rear porch before moving into the kitchen area.

Suddenly a loud, eardrum busting, crash sound occurred and scared the life out of me. I called out loudly for Stephanie or Derek and asked if they were alright. No answer. I shown the beam of the flashlight toward the spiral staircase and pointed it upward.

"Mr. Walker. Mrs. Walker," I called out, "are you folks upstairs? Are the lights out everywhere?" Again, no answer.

I heard a floorboard creak as if someone had just stepped upon it. I turned to focus my light on other areas of the first floor and heard the floorboard creak again.

"Is someone there?" I called out. "I have phoned the Police already, and they will be here any second." Still, nothing but silence.

As I turned to investigate another area of the house I heard a gunshot ring out and the sound of a bullet splintering wood off to my left. I quickly turned off my flashlight and pulled my cellphone out of my trouser pocket. Another gunshot rang out and this time the bullet was so close to my head that I heard the sound of it whizzing by. Time to duck and lay flat on the floor.

Before I could go prone, a third gunshot and this time the bullet caught me in my left shoulder and seemed to explode my bones and muscles into a hundred pieces. I cried out in pain and fell to the floor dropping my phone. Another gunshot and the floor boards next to me exploded into fragments.

Another gunshot, and the world starting drifting into an even deeper darkness. The pain of my left shoulder was becoming unbearable as it traveled down the left side of my body. "This is crazy" I thought, "This isn't happening to me. I have to..."

# CHAPTER 17

Derek and Stephanie couldn't believe what happened at their Victorian that night: the electricity being turned off and the lead-ins from the electric company being grounded so that it could not be turned on again. The house being ransacked on the first and second floors, and Mr. Walker being bound and gagged by an unseen intruder while poor Johnny Hamilton was shot and killed on the first floor by the same intruder. The police were 'dusting' every inch of the Victorian from the 'widow's walk' down to the basement for fingerprints, and any piece of evidence that they could find. Everything seemed to be clean; much cleaner than the police wanted to find it. Maybe, just maybe, Derek's new security system would shed some light on what went on inside the Victorian.

Carla was beyond grief stricken when she got the news of Johnny's murder, and completely collapsed. The medics had to revive her and help her regain her senses. Carl was so stunned that he nearly shut down and had to take a leave of absence from the bank. They both had to spend two days in the hospital before being allowed to go home.

Mrs. Walker went into shock when she returned home. She had been up in Boston attending the funeral of a close friend, and upon returning found both the murdered body of Johnny Hamilton, and the beaten and bound body of her husband. Mr. Walker had to spend four days in the hospital while being treated for his injuries.

It was Dr. Chambers who came to the family's aid. Dr. Chambers got those family members who needed hospitalization checked into rooms and looked after. It was also Dr. Chambers who offered to take care of the arrangements for Johnny's funeral and services when he found out that Carla was not capable of handling it. It was Dr. Chambers who suddenly became the family's 'white knight' by getting everyone the medical, and psychological help they needed, and a program of recovery for what they had been through.

In fact, were it not for Dr. Chambers, Derek, Stephanie, Carl, Carla, Mr. Walker, Mrs. Walker and Tom Kitchen would not have recovered as quickly as they did. Dr. Chambers saw to each and every one of them with personal visits, consultations with their doctors and virtually overseeing each part of their recoveries.

Oh, Tom Kitchen? Remember Tom is the owner of various businesses around Bridgeport including the 'About Time' clock shop. Seems Tom got some sort of minor infection and blood poisoning from wood splinters, and fragments. Tom also needed help with recovering from some type of gun powder burns.

Interesting…

www.ingramcontent.com/pod-product-compliance
Lightning Source LLC
Chambersburg PA
CBHW061548170626
46811CB00001B/132